CURSES AND CHAOS

1

ARCANE SOULS WORLD: THE LOST WITCH

ANNIE ANDERSON

CURSES & CHAOS
ARCANE SOULS WORLD
The Lost Witch Book 1

International Bestselling Author
Annie Anderson

Edited by Angela Sanders
Cover Design by Tattered Quill Designs

www.annieande.com

BOOKS BY ANNIE ANDERSON

THE ARCANE SOULS WORLD

GRAVE TALKER SERIES

Dead to Me

Dead & Gone

Dead Calm

Dead Shift

Dead Ahead

Dead Wrong

Dead & Buried

SOUL READER SERIES

Night Watch

Death Watch

Grave Watch

THE WRONG WITCH SERIES

Spells & Slip-ups

Magic & Mayhem

Errors & Exorcisms

THE LOST WITCH SERIES

Curses & Chaos

Hexes & Hijinx

THE ETHEREAL WORLD

PHOENIX RISING SERIES

(Formerly the Ashes to Ashes Series)

Flame Kissed

Death Kissed

Fate Kissed

Shade Kissed

Sight Kissed

ROGUE ETHEREAL SERIES

Woman of Blood & Bone

Daughter of Souls & Silence

Lady of Madness & Moonlight

Sister of Embers & Echoes

Priestess of Storms & Stone

Queen of Fate & Fire

To the ones that live in the grey.

I personally feel that no human is a hero or a villain. All of us have our grey sides...

— MANOJ BAJPAYEE

FIONA

My mama always said I'd catch more flies with honey than vinegar. That just showed what she knew. I seriously doubted when Mama was spouting the merits of honey and bees that she had murder in mind or was living in a world made of chaos. There was also a pretty good chance Mama hadn't been in the middle of a black magic spell to steal a boatload of power and damn the consequences, either.

Then again, she married my daddy, so anything was possible.

The spell I was in the middle of was a whole mess of vinegar, exactly zero honey, followed up by a little sewage for flavor.

You can do this, girl. Just breathe. This is the last one.

Internal pep talks were one thing, but there was little that could make me feel good about the dark magic I was polluting my veins with or what I would have to do next.

Two and a half years ago, an Unseelie Prince closed every single Fae gate in the world. Most cities were fine, the Fae populace so scant it had barely been a blip. Places like Savannah? It was *bad*. The Fae couldn't go home, couldn't see their families, couldn't access most of their magic. They turned feral—attacking any arcaner they could steal power from.

And worse?

My best friend was stuck on the other side of one of those stupid gates, trapped in the Unseelie realm with a king that wanted her magic for his own.

Wren Bannister was the only person on this planet that never looked down on me for being a Jacobs witch. Never gave me shit for my family or what my daddy did for a living. She'd saved my ass from certain death. She'd looked for me when no one else would. She never quit on me. And I'd be damned if I would *ever* stop looking for her—not until she was found, or I died trying.

It had taken a while, but we managed to find the prince responsible—not that finding him did a lick of good. It didn't matter that I'd trapped him in a cage so perfect that no one—especially my bosses—could sense him. It didn't matter that I'd crafted weapons especially for him—filled with magic, sweetening, and everything else I could think of to get him to break.

Nearly a year straight of interrogations and torture, and bargaining hadn't made a dent. He wouldn't cave. And if I didn't want the Alpha of one of the largest shifter packs in the South to lose his fool mind, I was going to have to do some things a fuck of a lot more drastic than I'd already done.

But the Acosta pack had taken me in, given me shelter when shit went sideways, and my best friend just so happened to be married to their Alpha. Getting his wife back to him had been at the top of my to-do list for every second she'd been gone.

And if the idiot prince in the Acosta dungeon wouldn't break, then I'd just have to break him myself.

The hard way.

The problem with the hard way? It had a bunch of consequences—ones only I would pay.

Swallowing hard, I tried to suck in a breath as I timed my steps just right.

This is the last one.

No coven in Savannah would help us. Trust me, I'd asked. No. I'd *begged.* My superiors, my contacts, anyone I could. No one would lift a finger to put an end to this. They didn't care that the Fae were stuck or that they were stealing magic from regular arcaners who'd never done anything to anyone. They didn't care that Savannah was changing for the worse day after day.

The ABI didn't give a shit, the witches couldn't give that first fuck, and the arcane community was at a standstill.

And I was trying to be good. Where I'd come from, what I'd done before I joined the Arcane Bureau of Investigation... I was trying not to be that person anymore. I'd done everything I could to not be the Jacobs Coven darling. To not be the enforcer my father made me to be, to not...

Someone once said that I was better than what my father made me to be—that I was better than him. Damn if I wasn't proving her wrong.

But there was no one to help, so I'd just have to do it myself.

I needed twelve deaths to get enough juice—twelve witch deaths, to be exact. A coven's worth of power was the only way I was going to be able to do this alone. I'd killed eleven people for this spell—a spell that made me no better than my daddy. That made me just as evil and debased as he had always wanted me to be.

Eleven.

And I needed one more. One more, and then I could take that Fae bastard's power. I could open the gates myself. Maybe not all of them, but I could open one. I could get Nico his wife back —my best friend back.

And then... then I'd...

Okay, so there wasn't a plan past opening the damn gate. If I stayed breathing after that, I'd wing it. I was good at that.

But it was one thing to kill in the name of self-defense. I'd done that before plenty of times. It was quite another to be combing files I only had access to as an agent for the Arcane Bureau of Investigation to pick out just the right targets. The ones with power, the ones with a dark past, the ones that had bought their way out of trouble. The ones that had gone free when they shouldn't have.

The ones that needed killing.

That was one thing I could say for myself. At least I was taking out the trash while doing something awful. It was more than my daddy could ever say.

Initially, I'd thought I'd do the world a favor and start picking off the Bannister clan. Wren's family was the worst. The problem was that the Bannisters had practically fallen off the map, hiding where no one could find them—not unless I wanted to break down their damn door.

So I'd combed the case files, looking for the worst I could find. And I found them all right.

All I needed was this last one, and I'd be done. I just had to not die in the process.

Mitchell Rhodes was a Rhodes Coven lieutenant—not that the Rhodes Coven was much nowadays. Almost extinct, they had damn near been run out of Savannah after some mysterious deaths. The ABI files told a different tale. Mitchy-boy was not just a murderer. He was a harasser, abuser, and a rapist. The only thing that had kept him out of prison was a very important friend on Savannah's Arcane Council and two cousins in the ABI.

I'd love to say that the ABI was any better than the human side of things, but I'd be lying my pretty little ass off.

One thing left out of the ABI files? Mitchell loved carousing human strip joints, abusing the employees, and then wiping just enough of their minds for them to know they were hurt but not be able to tell who'd done it. And if I timed my steps just right, I'd stop him in the act just this once.

"What the fuck do you think you're doing?" A rumble sounded from the dark recess of the doorway to my right, a familiar voice that should in no way be here. The athame in my hand was at Theo Acosta's gut before I ever really gave it the command to move.

Theo Acosta was the biggest pain in my ass, but

unfortunately, I couldn't get rid of him. As second in command of the Acosta pack, Theo had been in my business since the day we'd met. I'd managed to avoid him while in the middle of my little murder spree, but if he was here, the jig was up.

"I'm looking for a job," I quipped, tilting my head to the side like I was a little soft in the noggin. I mean, we were in a strip club, after all. "The ABI can't pay all the bills, you know." That was a bald-faced lie, but given my glamour and outfit, it sure as shit looked like the truth. How he could see through said glamour was a little concerning, but I couldn't think about that right then.

He gripped my wrist as he plucked the blade from my fingers like he was taking it away from a toddler, moving into the harsh illumination of the club's neon mood lighting. He'd gotten a haircut since I'd seen him last. His usual shoulder-length black locks were cropped close to his head in the back and left a little longer in the front, highlighting his strong jaw and fabulous cheekbones.

It suited him, *the bastard.*

I'd never met someone so pretty and so shitty all at the same time.

"Bullshit, Jacobs. You're up to something." The green of his wolf lit in his eyes, showing me just how pissed off he was. "You're always up to something."

In two and a half years, Theo hadn't trusted me one

bit—not that I'd given him a reason not to. He had some kind of beef with all witches—Wren excluded—so him warming up to me just wasn't going to happen. The rest of the Acostas loved me. Mari and I painted our nails together. Dayana and I shared dessert recipes. And his mama? She adored me.

But Theo? No such luck.

"Of course I'm up to something, you dope. I'm trying to get enough power to break the Fae in your dungeon, or did you forget about him while you were being so *judgy*? So why don't you go home, mind your business, and I'll get the answer to all our problems, mm-kay, Pumpkin?"

Those green eyes narrowed to slits as his jaw solidified. "Eleven witches are missing, Jacobs. No one has found the bodies, but I know they're dead. You planning a takeover? Expanding the coven for dear, old daddy?"

I ripped my wrist from his hold as well as the blade. "No, you moron. I'm getting enough power to make that Fae do what we need him to do before Nico decides to get himself killed. How many packs would love to take over Savannah, hmm? Five? Ten? And how well will your pack fare without a true Alpha when they come? How long do you think Nico will hold on without Wren?"

"Bull—"

The tip of my athame was at his throat in a blink.

"No coven will help me—help us," I hissed. "And no, I didn't ask my daddy for help because the last thing we need is Josiah Jacobs in Savannah." My father had pretty much taken over most of Tennessee and all of Kentucky. His fingers were in all the pies, he'd greased all the palms, and his hold was ironclad. Georgia would be next on his list if he even got a whiff of instability in Savannah.

I removed my blade and stepped back, my gaze drifting to the door where Mitchell Rhodes was about to lose his life. "This is the last one, and then I can... I can..."

My stomach churned. I associated dark magic with what I assumed a heroin addiction might feel like, you know, without all the high bits and keeping all the withdrawals. My bones hurt. I couldn't make myself eat anything. I was tired every second of every day. Breathing was a challenge. The likelihood I'd survive after this was damn near nil. But I wasn't going to tell Theo that.

I'd *never* tell Theo that. The fucker would probably throw a damn parade.

"In case you were wondering, the man I plan on taking out is a rapist and an abuser. They all were. I didn't take anyone innocent." I hadn't wanted to take anyone at all. I hadn't—

Theo inhaled a sharp breath through his nose, a low

growl building in his chest. "*Fine*, but watch yourself. This better not blow back on us, you got me?"

By "us," he meant the pack, and no matter what I'd done or how I'd helped, in his mind, that would never include me. Try as I might to ignore them, the words still stung. Two and a half years under Nico's protection, and Theo didn't think of me as anything other than a nuisance that helped occasionally. If he thought he could get away with it, he'd probably throw me off the closest cliff and be done with it.

And as if I would be so careless as to let anyone take the fall for my crimes. No, I was taking the brunt of the consequences on this one. As I should. If my wards had been better—if I would have protected Wren more—we wouldn't be here right now. She'd be safe, and I wouldn't...

Be a murderer? Don't lie to yourself, girl. You were living in the grey long before you started down this road.

I swallowed hard, ignoring the insidious voice in my head that had the audacity to tell the truth. "That's the plan." At Theo's resolute nod, I took a step away. "What? No lecture on how killing is wrong?"

Theo huffed, turning his back on me as he started down the hall. "That would make me a hypocrite, don't you think?"

Yeah, it probably would. Theo was no stranger to spilling blood. It was just usually at the end of his claws.

Well, I didn't have claws, so I'd just have to use what I could.

I watched Theo's back as he sauntered down the hall and out of sight, annoyed that he was working that suit for all it was worth.

Pretty but shitty, thy name is Theo.

Gritting my teeth, I slipped into the last room on the right where Mitchell was playing with his latest victim. According to the girls I'd spoken to, he started out tame as a pussycat before he pounced. Right then, his arms were stretched out along the back of the couch as a petite brunette slowly slipped out of her bra.

It seemed like I'd caught him just in time.

Waving my hand, I turned up the sweetening spell I'd perfected in my teen years as I slowly undid the buttons of my coat. Underneath was acres of pale skin and a skimpy emerald lace set. My glamour had me as a busty redhead with a rack that could be seen from space. I'd even changed my face a little, sharpening my nose and filling out my cheeks a bit to stave off that gaunt, dark magic look that was making eating a challenge. And Mitchell's eyes were exactly where I wanted them: on my overly inflated boobs.

"Well, look at what we have here," my mark muttered

as he widened his lips into an oily smile. "And it ain't even my birthday."

More like your death day, but who's counting?

Tilting my head to the side, I twirled a finger in my hair and bit my lip. "Oh, no, Sugar. The pleasure's all mine."

The dancer in between us shot me a confused look. Well, confused and a little pissed. I was horning in on her dance, but she didn't know what I was saving her from. Catching her hand, I yanked her to me and turned us so Mitchell wouldn't see me whispering in her ear.

"You want to leave this room," I murmured, turning up that sweetening spell so high it was possible she'd walk out of this room and never return.

She stumbled back, catching herself on her skyscraper heels before sweeping out of the room like her life depended on it. Funnily enough, it did.

"Hey, wait just a damn minute he—" Mitchell groused, but his tune changed as soon as I planted my ass onto his lap. He enjoyed one solitary second of my ass in his hands before my athame was at his throat.

Unlike Theo, Mitchell didn't have the skills or instincts to realize when he was in trouble, couldn't smell it on the air, or read it in my smile. And I wouldn't give this man the chance to change his circumstances. He didn't so much as gurgle before his throat was sliced from ear to ear, the blood draining out of him in a flood of scarlet.

Bile raced up my esophagus as I smeared the hot blood across his face, murmuring the dark magic spell that would lend me his power.

This is the last one.

Oily strands of magic lifted from his rapidly cooling skin, slamming into me with a force that knocked me off his lap. My blade went flying, and I struggled not to vomit all over the commercial carpet floor that was likely filled with a whole host of nasty things.

This is the last one.

Gritting my teeth, I swallowed a scream as fire lit in my bones.

This is the last one. No more. Just make it through this, and you're done.

And just like every other time I'd done this, I cursed myself for refusing to do the power exchange as my father would. I didn't perform the *other* spells that would ease this form of acquisition of power.

I didn't debase myself any more than I had to.

And this was why I wouldn't follow in my father's footsteps. I wouldn't crave power or money or favor. I would be...

Better? Girl, you're a murderer. How does that make you think you're better?

I was no better than Josiah Jacobs. No better than the man who was one tiptoe away from a full-on kingpin of the gods-be-damned Heartland.

Managing to peel myself from the disgusting floor, I cleaned up my mess, set myself to rights, and got rid of the body I now had on my hands. That was the *one* benefit of the magic I'd stolen—disintegrating a body was a snap. But it was only after the blood was gone from my skin and I'd opened the door did the real side effects set in.

The music from the club nearly split my skull as I made my way down the hall and out the back entrance, only managing to keep the contents of my stomach in until after I made it out into the hot, muggy night. To anyone else, I probably looked like some drunk party girl losing my lunch on the pavement. To an arcaner? I likely appeared precisely as I was—a witch with too much power and not enough sense.

But I had a Fae to break and a gate to unlock.

I just had to find the strength to do it.

2

THEO

There was nothing worse in my book than a witch who couldn't hold their magic.

Who was I kidding?

I couldn't stand the lion's share of witches on my best day, and I sure as fuck didn't care for the one right in front of me. It was bad enough that she came from a family that had ripped any chance of happiness away from me, but this particular witch?

She got under my skin in the worst of ways.

Fiona Jacobs wilted against the brick wall, her glamour falling away as dark magic lit her eyes with an inky blackness that made me fight off the urge to rip out her throat. Blonde hair hung in lank strands down her back, blending with her sallow skin that seemed to be pulled too tight over her bones. She wasn't eating, hadn't slept in years, and the magic polluting her veins was chewing through her faster than battery acid.

If she were anyone else, I wouldn't have thought twice about ending her right there and then. But Fiona was under my brother's protection, and I'd fucked him over enough over the last few years. Killing his mate's best friend?

That was liable to get me killed.

Hands tied, I stared at the pathetic witch, adjusting the cuffs of my shirt as I waited for her to finish vomiting up bile. If what she'd said in that club was true, she had just killed her twelfth witch in two weeks. I couldn't say her killing witches irked me. And her taking out ones that had gamed the system?

Even better.

What made my gut drop was the way she looked right then. She had enough dark magic in her to blow a hole in the world, and with the full moon in just a handful of hours, if she had it in her mind to fuck us over, she could do it with a simple snap of her fingers.

She heaved again and again, nearly falling on her ass as her knees wobbled.

For fuck's sake.

Like always, it would be me making sure another

Jacobs witch didn't burn the world down and all of us along with it.

"Are you planning on getting your shit together sometime soon?"

Taking her elbow, I hefted her to her feet, guiding us toward my car. At the tail end of winter, the nights were plenty warm enough to be just on this side of uncomfortable to anyone used to actual seasons. Damn, did I miss the ability to leave the city.

To head into the mountains whenever it suited me.

To escape.

With Wren gone and my brother half-insane, leaving the pack unsupervised was out of the question. Hell, leaving *Fiona* unsupervised was out of the question. The last thing I needed was her exploding herself to Kingdom Come and me getting blamed for it.

But knowing my luck with witches...

Fiona finally stopped her heaving, melting into a puddle in my passenger seat. Begrudgingly, I passed over a handkerchief so she could wipe her mouth. Her pale hand trembled as she reached for it, her bones practically rubbing together as she closed her fist.

"When was the last time you ate anything more than mints and coffee, Jacobs? Months? *Years*?" Grinding my teeth, I snapped the door closed, pinning this pathetic excuse for a witch in my car for some inexplicable reason.

Fiona was supposed to be looking for a way to help us —a way to get Wren back. But if she'd killed all those people to gain power, she sure as shit didn't seem to be able to use it. Hell, she could barely walk on her own.

"Do you have a plan?" I growled, peeling out of the parking lot. "Do you even have the faintest idea of what you're doing?"

Fiona's head lolled on the headrest, her pale-blue eyes staring me down. But she didn't say a word. Hell, she didn't even open her mouth. All she did was let her baleful gaze put me in my place as she struggled to breathe.

Fuck.

I'd seen plenty of dark witches in my time. Not a single one of them looked like Fiona did right then. The swirl of darkness to her power, yes. The lack of energy or strength? Hard no. Something was wrong with that woman, and I knew without a doubt in my mind I was going to take the blame.

Gritting my teeth, I pushed the car faster. I knew a couple of healers in the city. If I bribed them enough, they might even keep their mouths shut. The drive across Savannah was short, the silence only broken by Fiona's wheezing and moans. And all the while, the wolf that shared my brain howled at me to help her. It wanted to know why she was hurt and why she would do such a terrible thing to herself for the sake of the pack.

But Fiona was a Jacobs, and Jacobs witches only looked out for number one. Over the last three centuries, that coven had only ever been out for themselves, amassing stolen power and building an empire out of stolen land.

Fiona wasn't any different.

Josiah Jacobs raised that girl as an enforcer. Looking out for her coven was the only thing she was ever going to be able to do. And it didn't matter that my family loved her, and it didn't matter that she had caught them in her web.

She would be the end of us.

I was sure of it.

When we returned to the pack house, I spied my younger sister Mariella pacing before the front door. Stressed didn't seem to quite cover the emotions roiling off of her. She yanked at the hair at her temples, tears streaming down her face, one ear cocked toward the house so she could listen to whatever was happening inside.

Leaving Fiona inside the car, I stalked toward my sister, clamping my hands on her shoulders to make her stop pacing.

"What's wrong?" I asked, knowing full well what was

happening. No soundproofing in the world could dull the shouts and stabs and screams coming from the dungeon. Someone was getting the beating of their life down there.

Truth be told, unless it was Opposite Day, I couldn't seem to muster the give a fuck for the Fae bastard getting his ass handed to him. But Mari? She was losing her mind.

Not good.

"Nico's going to kill him," she moaned, wiping at the streaking mascara on her cheeks, only smearing it more. "Can't you hear it? He's lost his mind, and if he doesn't stop, he will beat Tristan to death."

Again, I couldn't see how that was a bad thing. If I were in my brother's shoes, I would have done it ten times over by now. There would be nothing left of that asshole other than pixie dust by the time I was done with him.

"I don't know what to do," Mari mumbled, shaking my hold off her shoulders. "I don't know how to stop him. I don't—"

"What do you care about some bullshit Fae prince? You know he's the reason Nico is half out of his mind. Why do you care?"

But I knew even without her telling me.

Nico might have some special mojo or whatever with the liminal spaces, but that didn't mean there wasn't a very good reason I'd been my father's right-hand man. My unique talent was inferring the bonds between people. I could tell you whether a family was strong or not. I could tell you if they were close to breaking. And faint as a whisper, there was a line floating into the house —and if I had a guess—it went all the way down to the dungeon and inside a particular cell.

"You didn't," I growled. Dumbfounded, I stumbled back a step to stare at my little sister. Nearly eighty years separated us, but I couldn't understand how she could be so fucking stupid. Wolves didn't get to just *pick* someone to love. Our mates were chosen for us—either by Fate or the universe or *whatever*. And Fate was just a cruel a mistress as the stories said.

She'd fuck you over in the blink of an eye. Mariella was just asking for heartbreak.

"I can't believe you would have the gall to fall for a Fae Prince. Are you kidding me?" Pinching my brow, I tried to stave off the migraine that was needling my brain. "You haven't even had the mating call yet, Mariella. You're really gonna hang your hopes on some asshole who likely won't survive the next twenty-four hours, let alone until the mating call hits you? And what happens when the call hits and it's not him?"

Because if Fate ever decided to be kind, it *wouldn't* be him.

"You're going to break your heart twice, little sister. You know that, don't you?"

Mari's wolf lit her gaze, the bright blue shining like a snow-covered tundra. "Caring whether someone lives or dies doesn't mean love, Theo. And if I did love him, it would be no business of yours, understand? It's been two years. If Tristan was going to break, he would have done it already. There's nothing that we can do to make him change his mind. He wants to keep his family safe. Wouldn't we all do the same? Truth be told, I don't even know if he *can* open the gates."

Perfect. Just perfect. I so loved it when my family lied right to my face. It was my favorite. "Bullshit. You haul off and fall in love with the prisoner in our fucking dungeon, and I'm supposed to clean up your mess? Is that it? I'm supposed to keep him alive so you can live out this fucked-up *Romeo and Juliet* fantasy of yours? Well, fuck that, Mari. Fuck. That."

Mari stumbled back like I'd just socked her in the gut, fresh tears spilling down her face as betrayal made a home there.

Gods, I was an asshole.

"No," she whispered, pressing a shaking hand to her chest. "I just don't want to hear Nico kill him. You have to stop him. *Please.*"

When did I become the glue that held my family together?

The door to my car opened, and Fiona practically melted from the passenger seat. Mari's eyes bugged a little, her pacing halted for a few seconds as she stared at Fiona in shock.

Great. I'm going to have to explain this shit, too.

Using the car to prop herself up, Fiona locked her knees and stood tall. The darkness still coated her gaze, but she seemed stronger than she had on our way over here. And it galled me to say that it gave me a little hope. I just needed a damn break already.

"I have a plan," Fiona said, her voice like ice over gravel. "But I need the Fae alive to do it."

Mari stared at Fiona like she'd never seen her before in her life, finally grasping what I'd been seeing this whole time. Fiona was broken—she had been for a long time. Well, that, and she was filled with enough dark magic to tear this whole world apart.

Fiona coughed a little, the faint scent of blood hitting my nose before it was gone.

Shit.

Jacobs seemed to gather herself, wiping her mouth with the back of her hand. "Stop your brother, Mari. If there's anyone he'd listen to, it'll be you. Calm him down, keep the Fae breathing, and I'll be down in a few minutes. Deal?"

Mariella peeled off, racing inside the house to stop my brother from doing something stupid. But I wasn't looking at my little sister. No, I was staring at the witch who looked like a stiff wind would blow her over.

"Okay, Jacobs. What's the plan here? You going to pick us off one by one, or are you just gonna steal a Fae Prince's power for your own gain? Did your daddy put you up to th—"

A bolt of dark magic slammed into my chest, knocking me on my ass. Pressure from Fiona's power crushed the breath right out of my lungs, and I would have set my wolf free, but she seemed to have a hold on both of us.

"You really need to learn when to keep your mouth shut, wolf. Or else one of these days, it's gonna get you into a heap of trouble you can't claw your way out of." Fiona's eyes bled from blue to black and back again, her jaw set in a hard line.

"I'm helping your family—something I've done every minute of every day since I stepped foot into this joint ages ago. You wanna be an asshole? *Fine.* Just stay the fuck out of my way while I fix this. Got it?"

I wanted to tell her to fuck off.

I wanted to rip her fucking throat out.

I wanted to let my wolf tear her to pieces.

But her magic was too damn strong. A moment later, it was as if a boulder had fallen off my chest. I gasped for air, finding my feet.

"You better know what you're doing," I growled once I caught my breath. "Because if you fuck it up, I'll be there to make sure you fucking pay for it."

Her spine straightened as she clenched her teeth. She passed me, her steps stilted like each one hurt her. She was damn near the entrance to the dungeon, but I heard her whisper as if her lips were at my ear.

"I'd expect nothing less."

3

FIONA

Bile burned in my gut as I tried to pull myself together. The last thing I needed to do was fall ass over tea kettle down these steps and break my fool neck. I gripped the railing, holding on for dear life.

"Please tell me that asshole is still breathing," I grumbled, eyeing the stairs that led down to the dungeon. "I doubt I could do a damn thing with his ashes."

That wasn't exactly true. I was sure they'd sparkle or something, and I could sprinkle them on Theo's head just to see if his whole body would explode.

Mariella was the youngest of the Acosta siblings and

far too rebellious for her own good. The girl thought in absolutes—absolutes that would get her into trouble one day. She respected family, sure, but she loved loyalty the most. Tristan had to have sold her the same line he'd been peddling to all of us. About how he was protecting his family above all else—no matter the consequences.

Sure.

Because nothing said devotion like fucking over an entire planet. Then again, nothing short of blind devotion to family would make Mari fall harder for him. He really was hedging his bets on getting out of here, now, wasn't he?

Mari positioned herself in front of the cell door like she was guarding it against Nico, and the Alpha himself was sweaty, bloody, and eyeing the Fae over his sister's head. Nico Acosta had taken the loss of his wife no better than I had. And that fucking Fae had just borne the brunt of his rage.

Tristan—or rather Drystan Haldrir Shadowfall, Crown Prince of the Dark Court—looked like he'd been put through a meat grinder. His long black hair was shorn to his scalp, the skin bloody in places and rough in others. His face was swollen and misshapen, his nose blooming like a damn rose. I'd feel sorry for the fucker if I didn't want to roast him over a spit and feed him to the rats.

Really, it couldn't have happened to a *nicer* guy.

"He is, thankfully," Mari answered, the relief so acute in her voice it almost made me hate the fucker a little less. Almost. "You really think you can pull this off?"

Maybe.

"Oh, yeah," I practically growled, showing my teeth as I eyed the Fae in the cage. "That gate is going to open, dammit. I don't care if I have to use your fucking entrails to do it."

Confidence I didn't feel fell from my lips, but bravado had gotten me out of just as many sticky situations as it had gotten me into, so I would just have to work it for all it was worth.

Tristan coughed out a wet chuckle, spitting a molar to the cement. "You overestimate yourself, witch."

If anything, the asshole had underestimated me.

He'd ruined everything. *Everything.*

My home out from under my father? *Gone.*

My career? *In shambles.*

My safety? *Crumbled to dust.*

He was lucky I didn't kill him myself.

"Fuck you, Pixie Dust," I snarled, damn near throwing myself against the bars. "You're just mad because your last bargaining chip is gone. I don't need you to open anything. Not anymore."

I'd made damn sure I had enough power for this one

thing, and damn if I wasn't going to make him eat those words.

Nico's shoulders drooped in relief, a renewed hope filling the dungeon. I fed off that confidence, letting it boost me up.

"What do you need?" Nico growled, but I didn't meet his gaze.

No, I stared the Fae down as I listed off everything I needed, watching with glee as fear etched itself into his face bit by bit.

Yeah, this fucker was toast.

Chatham Square was a small green space in the middle of Savannah, close to our old home. Hannah, Malia, Wren, and Nico had all lived in the four-story row house I'd purchased with my own money. It was my first home away from my father—my first chance to make a name for myself outside of the coven.

I was a newly minted ABI agent. I had friends. I had a future. I was free.

And that fucking Fae had ruined everything.

The city had been full of the little parks—vestiges of the battlegrounds of the vampire wars that made Savannah what it was today. Once upon a time—

before *someone* decided to close them all—they had been full of Fae gates, too. Wren had been tricked into one of them nearly three years ago, and she'd never returned. Tough to do when the damn things were sealed shut.

But I'd be opening them. I was sure of it.

I had sent Nico on a quest to get everything I needed to do the spell. Specifically, I needed the door to the cabin where the couple had sealed their mate bond.

That was a big enough ask—especially since Nico wasn't an agent anymore. But more? I needed Nico's blood, the Fae's blood, and... *Wren's* blood.

The only place on this plane where that still existed was a dried bloody carpet in the former Acosta Alpha's office. Wren had bled a lot in that room, and it remained untouched to this day. Plan B was to find Wren's mother and let her bleed out all over my spell—an option I was still considering.

As it turned out, the carpet was plenty enough—*pity*—and I didn't need to go on a wild Bannister goose chase.

Looking up from the bloody iron blade, I gauged the moon's position in the sky before studying my watch again. The face blurred for a second, and I had to blink hard to get my eyes to focus. "Okay, we need to wait until the moon hits its peak, and then I can start."

You can do this, girl.

As far as pep talks went, it wasn't much, but staying conscious while doing a spell far too big for my britches was about all I could ask of myself. I tried to think of it going right—of Wren walking through that door like these last two years, eight months, four days, and six hours had never even happened. That she hadn't ever been stolen. Like she was safe and whole and...

But I knew different, didn't I?

If I got Wren back from the Fae realm, the likelihood that she would be unharmed and whole was slight. If I got the gate open, that didn't mean the Fae would go back to normal, and even if all of the above *did* happen and Wren was safe, and the Fae quit being absolute shits, and Savannah yanked itself back from the literal brink, that didn't mean that my body wouldn't fail on me.

It didn't mean I'd live to see tomorrow.

It didn't mean that I wouldn't get my head chopped off because of the lives I'd taken.

It didn't...

You can do this, dammit. Now put your big girl pants on and get your ass in gear, girl. Time's a wastin'.

Swallowing down the fear that seemed to live in my gut, I made a beeline for Nico, the blade with Wren's blood still in my hand. While I had the power of twelve deaths just chilling under my skin, it had nothing on the energy radiating from just this little bit of blood. With any luck, her blood would be the key to opening the right door. With even better luck, it would bring her right to us.

And if we had a straight-up miracle, then everybody would survive this shit.

"It's time," I whispered, more to myself than Nico. "You ready?"

In answer, Nico held out his forearm, likely more than ready to get this show on the road.

Two years, eight months, four days, six hours, and twelve minutes. That's how long those doors had been closed. It had felt like decades.

Centuries.

Eons.

I brought the blade down, slicing through Nico's arm, mingling his blood with Wren's. Then I moved to Tristan, not bothering to give him the same care. Maybe it was his smile. Maybe it was his low chuckle that reminded me so much of Theo's. Maybe it was that he was the author of every failed moment of the last three years.

Or maybe it was the insult he mumbled in a language he didn't know I spoke.

"Cailleach dúr. Feicfidh tú deireadh mo lann sula bhfeiceann tú do chara."

Oh, I'm a stupid witch? We'll just see who meets whose blade first.

Brutally, I brought the knife down, wishing I could take his whole fucking hand with it. Smiling, I took his blood, relishing each howl of agony as I positioned myself in the middle of my circle. My grin grew as I watched his face register the chants falling from my lips in that asshole's native tongue.

And if I had a say, Tristan wouldn't live to see tomorrow, let alone long enough to kill me.

At the first revolution of the chant, the blade in my hand turned red-hot, scalding my skin with a blistering heat. Gnashing my teeth against the pain, I pushed forward, the ground beneath my feet rumbling with the first tremors of the spell.

The power in my gut roiled, aching to be used. A moment later, I let it off its leash, the rumbling turning into a full-on earthquake as the magic poured into the spell.

A door formed in the night, taking every splinter from Nico and Wren's door and making something entirely new. It seemed to spring up from the ground, its edges framed in dark thorns with sharp spikes. A curl of blackened vines topped it, at their center a grim skull with glowing rubies for eyes. Fire kindled at its base, the embers catching on the grass, blackening the wood and the ground, jumping from one blade to the next.

And this was when I felt the shift. I'd been aiming for

Faerie. I'd been aiming for Wren. But somehow, that dark magic had gotten away from me, spilling from my fingers, tearing from my bones, leeching everything I had stolen. I couldn't hold onto it—it was too much, too powerful, too...

I wanted to scream, to tell them all to run, to try and make it stop, but it was as if I was being hijacked in the worst of ways. The blade sizzled against my skin, but I couldn't drop it, and I couldn't stop the cadence of the spell from shifting to a language I didn't speak, to words I'd never said or heard, to a plea that should have never come from my lips.

An amber light backlit the door as it opened, the body-snatched chants petering out as it swung wide. At the fleeting glimpse of red hair, I nearly let the relief hit, but just as the world tilted on its axis, I quickly realized that the person walking through wasn't Wren. My whole body wrenched, the dark spell and all the spent magic turning on me as a tall, horned, bronze-skinned redheaded man strode through the opening.

Gold eyes scanned the square as the fire blazed across the grass, the iridescent scales on his bare arms shining in the light of the embers. His leather breastplate was covered in sigils I knew but had never drawn myself.

There was a very good reason witches were taught not

to dabble in that particular language—a language that had fallen from my lips not moments ago. Demonish.

Well, shit fire and save the fucking matches.

Agony brought me to my knees, and if I had a hope in hell, the magic would take me out before Theo did. Because I hadn't just failed to bring Wren back.

No, I'd opened up a Fates-be-damned gate to Hell. And all the while, I heard Theo's voice in my head asking me if I had the first clue what I was doing. I heard Tristan's bellowing laugh, taunting me. I saw the fear on Nico's face and heard the whispers of my father telling me I'd be back in the fold in under a week.

"You summoned a Prince of Hell by my blood. Where is my kin?" the demon rumbled, proving all my suspicions true.

If I weren't coughing up blood and begging for death, I would have laughed. I couldn't just fuck up small. *Oh, no.* I needed to fuck up so bad a Prince of Hell was on the mortal plane. I'd met one of his kind before back home, and they were no one to trifle with. It figured that I would fuck up so royally, I'd do this shit.

Go big or go home, right?

The flames flickered—or maybe that was just my vision—the light dimming, so I barely caught a glimpse of the white wolf tearing toward me across the square.

Yup, Theo would make good on his promise. I just hoped I'd be unconscious when he did.

And as the blackness swallowed me whole, I got the first stroke of luck I'd had all damn day.

I didn't even feel the teeth.

THEO

I couldn't recall a single time in my life that I enjoyed being proven right less than this one.

It didn't take a rocket scientist to know that a broken and weak Fiona wasn't up to opening the gate to Faerie. It also didn't take a genius to figure out that when her spell failed—*as I told my brother it would*—we would be in a world of shit.

Considering there was a seven-foot-tall Prince of Hell topside, I assumed my "I told you so" was self-explanatory.

Then again, had there been time to gloat, it would have been a different story. Too bad I was too busy hauling ass across the square. What I thought I was going to do against a Prince of Hell, I wasn't quite sure, but there was no way I was going to leave my pack without an Alpha.

Nico stood tall, his wolf roiling under his skin as the demon slowly approached.

Fucking idiot.

Without preamble, I put my shoulder in his gut and shoved him out of the way, putting myself between the demon and my brother.

"Get out of here, you asshole," I hissed, trying to get him to see reason. The truth was, Nico hadn't been able to see reason in years—which was probably why I got a solid punch in the mouth for my trouble.

Nico threw me aside like I weighed no more than a feather, the little prick drawing on his Alpha strength like the cheat he was.

"Where is my wife?" he growled, facing off against that damn demon like he was aching for death. "We never summoned you. We summoned her. Where the fuck is she?"

Understanding dawned on the giant's face as iridescent scales shifted on the skin of his arms. "Name her—your wife."

Slowly, I got to my feet, ready to yank Nico back—or hell, knock him out—if I had to. Spitting out blood, my gaze went to Fiona. Red stained her lips and chin, her gaunt frame practically withering to nothing.

Good riddance.

But a pang of worry twisted in my gut all the same. The Jacobs Coven had stolen everything from me, everything. I shouldn't give one ripe shit about a Jacobs witch, and yet... watching the blood trickle from her mouth made my whole body feel like I was dipped in ants.

"Wren Acosta," Nico answered, hauling my attention back to the matter at hand. His fists were clenched, his teeth bared, and we were about ten seconds away from him going full monkey shit and getting himself murdered.

Perfect approach, little brother. Why don't you beg him to eat us while you're at it?

The demon's smile was right out of a horror movie, his gaze meeting mine for a moment like he heard my thoughts somehow. "That is not the name she was born with, but you're right to cleave her from that lot. You need help finding her? I'll help."

Nico was a smart kid. With his time in the ABI, he knew good and well not to ever make a deal with a demon. But my little brother was not thinking clearly, and he sure as hell wasn't what I'd call "stable."

"Don't you fucking dare, Nicholas," I ordered,

grabbing him by the scruff of his collar. Yes, he was my Alpha. Yes, he could knock me into next week. But I'd lay down my life for the little shit a hundred times over before I let him make a demon deal.

"I ac—"

Don't ask what possessed me. Maybe it was the knowledge that Nico was not in his right mind. Maybe it was the literal demon wanting to make a deal. Without telling my fist to do so, I hauled him back and planted it in his jaw hard enough to knock him out.

Yeah, I'd pay for it later. I'd pay for a lot of shit later.

"Sorry to disappoint, but you won't be getting a deal out of my brother today." I adjusted his heavy body over my shoulder. "No offense, but if you could fuck off back to wherever it was you came from, that would be swell."

I dared to let my gaze slip to the side where Tristan used to be. Naturally, the Fae shithead was nowhere to be found.

It figured that I would be the one to clean up this mess. I'd been cleaning up my family's messes my whole life—a century's worth of mistakes just laid at my feet. Why wouldn't I clean up this, too?

"A summoning and no deal?" the demon huffed. "That hardly seems fair."

Personally, I didn't give a shit what he thought was fair. That didn't mean he was wrong, though. "Fair or not, my brother isn't of sound mind, and he should not be entering into any deals—demon or not." I shifted Nico just enough so I could stand in between the demon and the bloody witch at my feet. "Now, if you'll excuse us, we'll just be leaving."

He tilted his head to the side. "She summoned me? That little thing? I'm intrigued."

His words shouldn't have pissed me off, but they did.

"Intrigued or not, you're not getting either of them. You weren't the one we wanted to summon. We wanted your *kin* or whatever, so you'd be doing us a huge favor if you would go back to wherever it was you came from and let us try and find her ourselves."

King of negotiations, I was not. I had never been what one would call "smooth." My father only brought me in when the talking was done, and personally—not that I'd ever tell him so—it was one thing I admired my brother for.

He could talk to people.

I could only kill them.

The Demon Prince tilted his head to the side, surveying me in a way that made me not at all comfortable. "You cannot find my kin. It seems you need help with that. I have many who will help me. Shall I call them?"

That sounded like the worst idea ever. "No—"

The ground vibrated beneath my feet. The last time it had done that, Fiona summoned a gate straight from Hell. My gut told me not good things about this new little rumble.

Moments later, that tiny, little rumble was a full-on earthquake, knocking me off my feet and making me drop my brother. Holding on to the ground for dear life, I watched as blackness busted through the door in a cloud of murky whispers and buzzing.

Not good, not good, not good.

The demon's smile was again straight out of a horror movie. "If you cannot find her, we will."

My brain supplied words like incorporeal and possession, but I was still clinging to the ground as it shook with the force of the power leaking like a sieve from the door. And then, the fucker winked out of sight, taking his cloud of what had to be demons with him.

Wind and fire whipped through the square, jumping from one tuft of grass to the next, engulfing whole trees in one violent gust. Fiona coughed at my side, her skeletal frame peeling itself off the ground like she had no energy left. Blue eyes widened to saucers as she took in the blaze nearly surrounding us.

"What happened?" she whispered, her voice slurring as she finally made it to her feet.

Unable to hold the wolf under my skin, claws erupted from my fingertips as I snatched my brother from the ground, redepositing him onto my shoulder.

What? Was he made of lead or something?

"Your fucking mess—that's what happened. It's what happens when you don't know what the fuck you're doing. You talk a big game, Jacobs, but when it comes to real magic, you don't have that first clue. Now we have a gate to Hell open, no way to fix it, and a Prince of Hell on the loose. Congratu-fucking-lations."

Now the entire city would burn down all because she thought she was Queen Hot Shit with a gods-be-damned wand.

"You have a plan for the blaze that's gonna kill us in the next twenty seconds?" I did my best not to choke on the thick smoke pouring from the blazing trees but didn't quite manage it. And unless I wanted to run through flames, there wasn't exactly a way out of here.

A frown puckered her brow as wispy white light trailed from her fingers. Gritting her teeth, she seemed to press her hands into the blaze, driving it away from us. And while I appreciated the fresh air, there was still the matter of a whole park on fire in the heart of the city.

Fiona stumbled to a knee, blood pouring anew out of her nose as she whispered pained words in a language I didn't know. Coughing, she spat blackened blood to the dirt before she gasped a watery breath. For a moment, the flames seemed to freeze their hungry path across the treetops, but the cost seemed a bit too steep.

She gasped again, the air not quite meeting her lungs as it whistled in her throat and got stuck. Even over the roar of the flames, I knew Fiona was just about as close to death as someone could get and still be conscious.

It was bad enough my brother was unconscious, and at any minute, the ABI would show up and cart us all off to jail. Now she was just gonna die on me?

I don't think so.

With nothing for it, I let my talons free, digging them into my brother's side in the hopes of waking his dumb ass up. The effect was instantaneous. Nico shoved off my shoulder, landing in a crouch on the ground, his fangs and talons at the ready.

His golden eyes, hinting at his wolf's desire to rip my throat out, made me step back.

"What the fuck, Theo."

I wanted to rage, but the best I could do was point at the obviously dying witch at our feet. If the fire department wasn't coming, the ABI was probably already on their way. The lack of sirens, in this case, was doubly bad.

"Heal her, dipshit, before she dies on your watch. I know you can."

My brother had once healed his wife right before my eyes, an ability there hadn't been in an Alpha in centuries. She'd been dying in his arms, and even though that particular power could bring a world of hurt to him and our entire pack, he'd still healed her. I knew without a doubt then that he loved her more than life. From then on, I knew I would do whatever it took to make sure that he never lost her again.

Nico's gaze loosely focused on Fiona. *I must have hit him harder than I thought.*

"Any day now, little brother."

It was almost as if my own lungs were burning for oxygen, my own heart slowing, my...

Fuck empathy, you asshole. Focus.

With a touch of his hand, Fiona's breaths evened out, which was about all we could do under the circumstances.

"Time to move," I growled, sensing figures moving in the night past the stagnant wall of flames. Fiona hadn't been able to extinguish the blaze, but damn if she hadn't stopped it from spreading. But flames or not—we were liable to be in a world of shit if we stayed.

Nico stumbled as I lifted Fiona over my shoulder.

"I can't carry you both, so get your shit together, asshole."

Narrowed gold eyes sliced to me. *Yeah, I'm gonna pay for that later.* But what was I supposed to do? The only thing for it was to wake him all the way up.

"That demon prince? He let a whole legion of incorporeals out with him. We need to get under cover before—"

The truth had the intended effect. Nico sobered instantly, fists at the ready, his gaze focused.

"Right. Home first. Demons later."

The slog back to the pack house was rife with too many people and not enough darkness, but we managed not to get beheaded or snatched up by the ABI. Tricky, considering I had an unconscious woman over my shoulder and probably smelled like burnt hair and spent magic.

The front door to our family home never looked so good. I hadn't lived there in years, but damn if the place didn't seem like the safest spot in all of Savannah.

"Put her in the basement," Nico growled, his jaw clenched tight as he shoved through the front door. He meant the dungeon, but far too kind to actually say it. "In the null cell. We need her magic hidden as soon as possible. Before—"

But he didn't even finish that sentence. I might not

have been able to stomach Fiona Jacobs dead, but in a cell?

That, I could do.

One flight of stairs later, and she was locked up tight right where she belonged.

5

THEO

I never expected that while I was relishing Fiona's inherent downfall, that she would end up the actual bane of my existence.

It took twenty minutes for my brother to drop the hammer on me. Granted, I was actually amazed it had taken him that long. I had knocked out my Alpha and carried him around like a rag doll.

I should be dead.

Personally, I'd take the death sentence over the babysitting job I'd been saddled with.

"You have got to be fucking kidding me," I growled, ready to knock my brother into next week. Again. "You were about to make a deal with a Prince of Hell. What the fuck was I supposed to do? Let you sell your soul? Let you make a demon deal? Kiss your ass goodbye?"

Nico's jaw solidified to granite as his wolf roiled under his skin, a sign I might have been pushing him too far.

"I am not punishing you, Theo," he ground out through clenched teeth, each word enunciated like I was testing his patience. "You are my second, and I am making sure you are doing the job that needs you the most. The ABI will be looking for Fiona."

"As they should." I ripped a hand through my newly short hair before yanking my suit jacket from my shoulders. "She opened a gate to Hell, Nicholas. Of course they should be looking for her. They should arrest her. Fuck, they should probably behead her. And you want me to play babysitter to this fucking menace? You know this is bullshit."

Nico pinched his brow. "Again, this is not a punishment. This is what I need you to do, and I swear to everything holy, if you keep fucking pushing me, I'm going to pay you back for knocking me out. Now do me a favor and just do the gods-be-damned job I'm telling you to do."

Fitting two fingers into the tie at my neck, I loosened the fabric enough for me to breathe. "We should have left her there. You know that."

Nico's mirthless chuckle was half-insane, half-resigned. "It wasn't my idea to heal her, and it wasn't me who picked her up and carted her back here, you dumbass. Borrow a clue, pretty please?"

It really pissed me off when my brother had a point.

"So, what? I sit here and watch her detox from black magic and…" I trailed off, not exactly wanting to alert my brother to the other problem I'd discovered. *Ah, fuck it.* "You know what she did to get that magic, don't you?"

I didn't know how exactly I would tell my brother about the twelve murders under Fiona's belt, but somehow, I'd find a way.

Nico turned, heading for the stairs. "Of course I know what she did. I know you think I don't know what's happening in this city, but I do. Probably better than you. She sacrificed a lot to get that door open. I don't know why a demon stepped through, but I'm not blaming her."

"Well, if you won't, I will," I muttered, unbuttoning the top of my no-longer-white shirt. Fiona had bled all over me, and I'd never get the stains out.

"She did everything that she could, and she failed. But she's under my protection, and you will treat her with respect." A wisp of a smile broke out over his haggard face. "That is your punishment."

I really hated being right. Of course, he'd saddle me with the albatross of the universe for knocking him out.

Of fucking course he would. "Oh, come on. This is bullshit."

"Sack up, *Mrs. Doubtfire*. You've got a job to do."

I sliced my gaze to the pitiful-looking woman sleeping on the hard concrete of the null cell. She'd been unconscious for the last hour while we made our way through a demon-infested city back to the pack house. She hadn't so much as twitched.

She needed a blanket, at least. Maybe some food. That was if she could even keep it down. I wasn't a witch, but the null cell still made my stomach turn. No idea what she'd do when she woke up. Then again, detoxing from a coven's worth of dark magic would probably kill her no matter what I did to make her more comfortable.

"Are you sure you even healed her enough?"

"Could you tell me what you actually want in this scenario? Do you want me to heal her, or do you want me to leave her in Chatham Square so she could burn to death? You're gonna have to make up your mind."

Gritting my teeth, I fought off the urge to punch my brother in the face for a second time. Nico being right irritated the absolute shit out of me.

"Just trying to make sure she doesn't die on my watch."

"And I'm trying to make sure the rest of us don't follow her."

And that sobered me right out of my bullshit pity party. It was bad enough that I had lost the Fae Prince. If we got caught while I was bitching about watching Fiona, I'd never forgive myself.

"Fine. I'll watch her. It's not like she's doing anything, anyway." That didn't mean I loved being cut out of the fight should there be one. Reaching out, I squeezed his shoulder. I wasn't a hugger, but Nico needed someone—anyone—to keep an eye on him. I'd have to send a text to Wyatt if I could get service down here. "If you need me, I'll be here."

"Thank you," he said on a sigh, the fight seeming to leave him for a moment. "I know it's not your fault that he escaped, but I can't think about that right now. Do me a favor and keep her alive, please? We may still need her to get out of this."

His old boss Serreno had already called, I didn't know what she said, but it was enough to put my brother on red alert.

"The ABI are going door-to-door. Apparently, the Demon Prince let out thousands of demons. I'm pretty sure she knows it was us, too."

Fuck. Serreno was a rule-follower to the nth degree. We weren't just fucked. We were *fucked.*

"They're searching for the power signature that

opened that gate. Keep Fiona in the null, keep her alive, and we'll figure this shit out."

Not that it was ever in my control to keep Fiona alive, and if the ABI looked even a little at our home, we would be screwed.

Nico started up the steps, his back to me, but I still heard the whispered words all the same. "There's still a chance that we can get Wren back."

And while I knew that would always be at the forefront of Nico's mind, Wren wasn't a concern for me.

Our pack was.

"And I'm going to need you to realize that our pack—the people that follow you—are more important right now. I've already gone through one Alpha failing to see that. I'm not going to do it a second time. Get your shit together, brother, or I'll knock you out and do it for you."

Nico sobered, pulled out of the spiral of awful thoughts that had to be plaguing him right then. We had just lost his best shot at finding his wife. Eventually, he would realize that. Eventually, he would mourn.

I just hoped that he would actually be our Alpha in the meantime.

Without another word, he stomped up the steps, my dismissal evident as he slammed the dungeon door closed. It seemed I was the deliverer of hard truths today.

It wasn't more than thirty minutes before I heard

stirring in the cell. Naturally, it wasn't enough time to get Fiona a blanket or a pillow or food. The best I could come up with was a glass of tepid water from the bathroom sink. Reluctantly, I took the keys from the hook and opened her cell.

A shivering Fiona peeled her eyes open, her face stained with blackened blood and her eyes half-lidded.

"Here, drink this," I offered, crouching to her level. She'd coughed up enough blood to fill a well. She had to be thirsty—healing or no healing.

She eyed the glass. "Is it poison?"

If only I was that lucky.

"If I was going to kill you, I would have left you for dead in Chatham Square. Drink it, don't drink it. I don't give a fuck." Gritting my teeth, I stood, turning to leave the cell that made my stomach churn.

"You sh-should have j-just k-killed m-me," she croaked, her voice like broken glass as she struggled to speak.

That stopped me cold. I cut my gaze to her, watching as the violent shivering got worse. She needed to get off that floor. She needed heat. She needed…

"What did you just say?" I didn't stick my neck out saving her ass—*twice*—for her to wimp out now.

"The ABI w-will be c-coming for me." She curled in on herself, her bloody hair mingling in the dried pools of

Fae blood that my brother had spilled just hours earlier. "Y-you should have le-left me there like I know you w-wanted. I si-signed up for t-that."

She might have earned this cell, but death? *Yeah, yeah, it still stuck in my craw.*

"I k-knew what I was getting in-into when I opened th-that gate, Theo. It d-doesn't matter how lo-long you keep me in this c-cell. They're g-going to find me."

She wanted me to kill her—I could see it in her eyes. She wanted death—maybe even thought she deserved it.

Maybe she did.

But I wasn't going to be the one to do it.

Snatching my jacket off the back of a metal folding chair, I returned to her cell, covering her with the bloody fabric. It was the best I had, and it pissed me off. I almost left her there.

Almost. But before I could leave, something tugged at the recesses of my humanity.

Grinding my teeth, I picked her up off the floor, depositing her on my lap as I let the heat of my body warm her.

"Detoxing is going to be a bitch. You're liable to break a bone shivering that hard." *Yeah, the argument was weak. I'd have to do better than that.* "Nico still thinks you're worth saving, so you're staying alive, got it?"

Fiona eyed me with a baleful glare. "N-nico isn't

always right, y-you know. It w-would be better f-for the pack if I w-wasn't here."

She wasn't wrong, but that didn't mean I would disobey my brother. As shitty as it was, he was probably right this time. Abandoning a member of the pack—no matter how tenuous—was one of the worst things a wolf could do.

"Well, he told me to put you in this cell, and he told me to keep you alive, so that's what I'm doing."

Her shivers only got more violent as time went on. Without telling them to do so, my arms circled her shoulders, and my hands tried to warm her fragile skin. And I was so busy worrying whether or not she would go into shock in this shitty cell, that I didn't hear my brother and sister come down the stairs.

Not until it was too late to pull myself away from her.

"Well, lookie here," my little brother Frankie jeered, his ineffable smile wide on his face.

There had never been a time any of my siblings had seen me with a woman. I was over a century old and hadn't brought a single woman home to the family. Maybe it was because my mate had already died. Maybe it was because I knew I'd never get married. Hell, I didn't even hug, for fuck's sake.

But here I was, holding a witch in my arms like it was just another Tuesday.

Fuck.

"I don't want to hear shit," I whispered, trying not to wake her. At some point, Fiona had passed out, still shivering in my arms as the detox started in earnest.

"What? I didn't say anything. You just look so cute there cuddling, I just couldn't help myself."

In his arms was a collapsible cot and mattress, and behind him was his twin, Ella, with a plate of food in one hand and a bundle of bedding under her other arm. On her face was a shit-eating grin, but unlike her twin, she was smart enough not to say anything.

She set the plate on a tool cabinet, eyeing the woman in my arms like she didn't know what to make of the situation. "Mom is bringing everyone in, but she wanted to make sure Fiona was comfortable down here. Looks like we need to bring in another cot?"

Frankie snorted, his stupid grin getting bigger. "Or maybe they can share this one."

"Fuck off, Frankie," I growled, ready to set Fiona down and make him eat those words.

His expression sobered, but I could tell he was holding in a laugh. "Yes, I can see that you would like some time alone." He set the cot on the stone floor and began assembling it. "I'd let you do this, but you seem busy."

Ella barely held in a snort. "I hope you don't mind,

but since Mom is calling everyone in, they sacrificed your room to have a bunch of the younger pups bunk together. You're stuck down here, buddy."

And Nico said that this wasn't punishment.

"Do I get a cot," I muttered, trying to hold in my growl, "or has Nico decided I'm sleeping on the floor?"

Frankie's face sobered for real this time, worry puckering his brow. "That depends on if we survive the night."

After my siblings left, I was once again alone with a shivering, detoxing Fiona in a cell that made my gut pitch. The only upside was we were on a cot off the frigid floor. As her trembling got worse, I wrapped her in blankets and did my best to ignore the creaking of her bones and the way her teeth chattered against a chill only she felt. I'd never seen a witch detox from that much magic, but I couldn't imagine it would be pretty.

It wasn't long before a booming knock on the front door set my teeth on edge. Nico had said the ABI was coming, but a part of me never believed it. A part of me never thought they'd scramble so fast to show up here. The commotion upstairs was loud enough that it seemed like I was on the first floor in the middle of it.

Nico said they were going door-to-door, which meant they didn't know where the magic came from and possibly couldn't even pinpoint who had done it. If that were true, there was a possibility that the pack would be safe even with Fiona here.

"Nobody move," a woman barked once Nico opened the door, the thumps of footsteps rattling my bones. "Director Erica Serreno of the ABI. I have orders from the Council to search this home. Do you comply?"

My brother's sigh was loud enough that I could hear it all the way down here. Erica was his old boss. No way he wanted her in his home with a bunch of agents they scrounged from the dregs. "You know you don't have to announce yourself, Erica. You are free to search this home, but please keep in mind every single person under this roof is under my protection. As such, none shall be harmed without consequence. Make sure your officers know that."

A part of me breathed a sigh of relief. Nico was acting like an Alpha—a real one. The other part knew what most agents thought about shifters in general. They'd probably take it as a threat.

"Alpha privilege doesn't work right now, Nico," Serreno muttered. I couldn't see her past the door, but her voice was significant enough to carry. "Someone opened a gate to Hell. If we find out it was your pack that did it, there's nothing I can do and no law that will save you."

My stomach roiled as I paced the cell. We were fucked, no two ways about it.

"Fair enough."

The whimpers from young pups made my skin itch as boots clomped all over the floors above. There was nothing I could do if I went upstairs now. The agents would know there was a dungeon in this house. I would give away Fiona's position and, in turn, damn us all.

There was nothing to do but sit and wait and pray they didn't find the hidden door.

After several minutes of nail-biting waiting, the worst words I'd ever heard came.

"Getting a power signature, Director," an agent said, his voice far too close to the dungeon door for my comfort.

Was it possible that he could feel Fiona even though she was under a null ward?

"Are you sure?" Serreno asked, their voices coming closer and closer.

My gaze tracked to the open cell door.

I was a fucking idiot. The null wasn't complete because the door was sitting wide open. Gritting my teeth, I forced myself to leave Fiona on that cot wrapped in blankets, forced myself out of the cell, and—against my better judgment—I closed the door on her, completing the null and sealing her in.

Fists clenched, I readied for them to come down those stairs—the urge to fight, the urge to claw and tear and rip filling my gut. My wolf whispered words of malice, of murder, and I knew if they came down those stairs, I would tear someone apart.

I knew that if someone tried to take her, I would do just about anything, and that confused me more than I thought possible.

"Wait," the agent said, confusion coloring that single word. "It's gone. I could have sworn..." His words trailed off for a moment, making the breath in my throat catch. "I could have sworn there was something behind this wall with the same power signature as whoever opened that gate."

There was a long pause that nearly made me come out of my skin.

"Maybe they're outside? It's possible that they're moving. Pack everyone up. We need to follow it."

As the thunder of feet and shouted commands faded, the house was once again silent.

But even with that silence, it didn't help my confusion one bit.

6

FIONA—ONE MONTH LATER

Whoever the sadistic bastard was that constructed this null cell deserved to be publicly shot.

Oh, wait.

That evil genius was me.

Too bad public executions were off the table.

I didn't know exactly how long I'd been in here, but my best guess was around a month. As far as I could tell, it had taken me over a week to get over the worst of the black magic withdrawals. In the process, Nico had to heal me four times just so I would survive. I missed a lot during that time, and it wasn't as if my jailer was forthcoming with the details.

Theo Acosta had made good on his promise to hold me accountable if my spell failed. At least I couldn't call the man a liar on that front. I hadn't seen the sunshine or taken a breath of fresh air in more days than I could count.

Nico said it was for my own good, but I knew better.

This was a punishment that I deserved—probably too good of one, to be honest.

That wasn't to say I felt like the prisoner I most definitely was. They did their best to make me comfortable.

The first order of business was putting in a shower and a toilet and giving me a decent amount of privacy behind a beautiful rice paper screen. I hadn't been conscious for any of that, but when I finally woke up over a week later after my disastrous Hell gate snafu, there it sat, the gorgeous gold- and peacock-blue design, the only bright spot in this gods-forsaken dungeon.

Over the coming days, someone had installed a TV, a couch, and a cute little table filled with a wealth of cosmetics and things to keep me busy. There were decks of cards, board games, sudoku books, hardbacks, and an e-reader filled with every single romance novel known to mankind already loaded onto the device.

My favorite of all the gifts was a forest-green velvet couch that sat on a plush rug. It warmed the area in a way most things couldn't. Sure, it was Savannah in springtime, so the temperature should be three degrees past boiling, but down in the damp, dank dungeon, I was always cold.

Wrapped in sweatshirts, jackets, and blankets, I always seemed to be just shy of freezing, the null bars doing nothing to help.

Those things always seem to simply appear.

One moment I'd be sleeping, and the next, I'd wake to a new trinket or piece of furniture in my space. If I didn't know better, I would think it was Theo leaving them, but I did know better. The Acosta family—*or most of them*—loved me. That didn't mean that I was okay down here with them doting on me—I wasn't—but I'd already caused enough trouble.

A week or so ago, Dayana helped me dye my hair for the first time in maybe ten years. I'd been my father's perfect little enforcer for so long that I couldn't remember the last time I'd done something for myself. Well, save for joining the ABI and telling him to shove it. Dying my hair was a final rebellion for me—a way to differentiate myself from the perfect little princess image he always suggested.

I loved designer clothes, and I loved cute shoes and

handbags, and jewelry. I loved it all, so having to dress nice had never been a hardship, but it was always those backhanded compliments that did me in. He and my mother were just a little too in the middle of my life, had too many opinions about every little thing I did.

Dying my hair, even at thirty-eight, was still a tiny rebellion. Then again, it might have just been the color.

I twirled a purple rope of hair around my finger, letting the low light of the dungeon glimmer off the strand. Dayana had done a beautiful job. There was a little bit of blue, a little bit of fuchsia, and a whole lot of purple. For some reason, I'd always wanted purple hair, and the way the color complimented the green of the couch made my heart swell.

But not even pretty-colored hair could keep me from wanting to climb the walls after a month. It didn't matter how many books were on the tablet, or how many movies I had access to, or how many crossword puzzles and sudoku games I'd won, I was bored to tears.

Bored out of my skull, and the only thing I could play with was Theo's mind.

Settling onto the couch cushions, I eyed my prey. The eldest Acosta brother was the most uptight, pain in the ass man on the planet. Don't get me wrong, I had dealt with many a man before and had my fair share of assholes, but Theo was the King Poo-bah of the Proctology Brigade.

Maybe it was that he was always in a suit. Maybe it was because he never thought before he opened his mouth. Or maybe it was just that he absolutely hated me. Then again, it could have been a combination of all of the above.

"You've been stuck down here for a month. I know why I'm here, but what did you do to get saddled with my babysitting gig?"

It hadn't occurred to me until just then that, other than changing clothes and maybe taking a shower, Theo hadn't left this dungeon as long as I'd been there. Now, I was used to the odd way the Acostas punished each other, but relegating the eldest brother to jailer didn't seem to make sense.

Theo turned the page on an old beat-up western he'd been reading for the last hour. "Who else is going to watch your crazy ass? I know you had to have studied each and every bar and lock on that cell. Hell, you created the damn thing. Eventually, you'll figure out a way to break out of it—magic or no magic. And I will be here when you do."

I knew the scent of bullshit when I smelled it.

"You're scared I'm going to break out, even though I haven't so much as twitched toward that door in a month? You and I both know that if I get out of this cell, the ABI will take my head. And while you're probably fine with that, it doesn't quite leave me the motivation to bust out."

That said, I really missed not being under these bars. It was my obsession—the feeling of my skin not under a null ward.

Not that I would get it anytime soon.

"Sure you don't," he muttered, flipping another page. "And the feeling of the ward on your body isn't bugging you one bit. Is that why I have to basically force-feed you? Because, let me tell you, that's the highlight of my day."

Theo wasn't lying. Eating had become a chore under the wards, just as it had been in ABI school. But the problem was that the school, with its wide-open spaces, didn't have wards nearly as strong as mine. This cell was built with a certain Fae Prince in mind, not a witch. And because I had tuned these bars specifically for his level of power, the juice was a little too much. A coven's worth of power or not, it didn't begin to compare with my cell's former occupant.

It was tough to eat anything when your stomach wanted to claw itself out of your body.

I waved my hand, wiping his words away. "Enough about me. I want to know why you're down here.

Because your answer is complete bullshit, and we both know it. Come on, what did you do?"

Sitting forward, I speared him with my gaze, not even blinking. Theo hated to be stared at. *Hated* it. Watching him squirm was glorious, but today I was getting answers.

"Nothing," he grumbled, turning another page as he adjusted in his seat.

Fidgeting already? Weak sauce.

"You realize I have nothing but time, right? I can't go anywhere, and it seems you're just as stuck as I am. Which means you're trapped with my inquisitive ass until you answer me. I don't think you've realized just how annoying I can be when I don't get my way." Smiling evilly, I steepled my fingers. "What did you do?"

"Noth—"

Oh, please. He isn't getting off that easy. "I will annoy it out of you. You think I haven't seen how pissy you get when I paint my nails or spritz perfume? I've been actively trying *not* to annoy you. Imagine what I'll do when I actually put my mind to it. You know you wanna tell me. What is it?"

Eye twitching, he tried to ignore me for a few more seconds before he slammed his book closed. "Fine."

At first, I thought he was going to get up and leave. Unlike me, he could actually make a break for the place.

But when he rotated in his seat to actually face me, I knew I had won.

Trouble was, he refused to meet my eyes. *Interesting.*

"There are several reasons why I am down here." He ticked off the first with his index finger. "One, I may or may not have knocked Nico out before he could make a deal with the demon." He held up his second finger. "Two, I may or may not have been party to Wren's almost-execution, and three, Nico and I have never really gotten along."

Did he think he could just sandwich the meat of the situation between two flimsy pieces of bullshit, and I wouldn't notice?

"Whoa, whoa, whoa," I barked, climbing to my feet. "You're telling me you were part of hurting Wren? You low-down dirty piece of sh—"

Green lit his eyes as he abandoned his chair, too. "Shut your mouth. You don't know the first thing about it." He let out a mirthless chuckle as a hint of an emotion I couldn't place crossed his features. Maybe it was pain, but something told me it wasn't.

Regret. Self-loathing. Helplessness.

"And I know you don't have the details, because if you did, you'd know my father took our will away. My father had a penchant for taking away someone's choices if he thought they would disobey him. He couldn't do it to Nico, but that didn't stop him from doing it to the rest of us."

My heart dropped, and my stomach churned. I'd never thought Theo and I were anything alike until right at that second. I'd never recognized a single thing we had in common other than liking designer clothes. But it sounded like Theo's father and mine were far more similar than I'd care to admit.

Slowly, I lowered myself back to the couch, a lump forming in my throat.

"Okay," I murmured, trying not to let my voice tremble, "you're right. I don't know a damn thing about it. But I'd love to hear whatever you have to say."

"It's why Nico killed him, you know. Because he forced us. It nearly tore my family in two, what he did." Theo reluctantly retook his chair, his fingers tugging at the insufferable tie that always seemed wrapped around his neck. "My father said it was the only way for Nico to survive. Wren was cursed, and their bond was taking him down with her. Even though most of us didn't want to, Dad used his power to make us. Nico knows we didn't have a choice, but I think part of him still blames us. Blames me."

That pissed me off. "From what I gather, you didn't have a choice—none of you did. Nico doesn't blame the others. Why would he blame you?"

"No," he said on a sigh, "we didn't, and resisting an Alpha's will is not easy. Many of us don't have the strength. But none of the others held a knife to his wife's throat. I'm lucky he hasn't killed me by now."

That brought me up short. I remembered Wren coming home shell-shocked and bloody, her fingers tracing her neck like she was afraid a wound would open there. I had wanted to roll some heads, but I couldn't exactly start a war with the whole pack. Plus, Nico had handled that problem himself. I could see now how there would still be an element of dissension between the brothers.

I could see a future where if we didn't get Wren back, Nico could continue on down his path of insanity. I could see a time where his leniency toward Theo might change. From the snippets I'd heard from Nico's sisters, he was losing more of himself every day.

"Luckily, my little brother is different from our father. He would never take our will away, but that leaves us room to fuck up."

And free will was a consummate bitch.

7

THEO—THREE MONTHS LATER

The streets of Savannah were nothing like the ones I'd grown up with. A hundred-some-odd years ago, most of them were either dirt or cobblestone. Now they were asphalt ruins filled with burned-out cars and debris. Taking one of the few breaks I ever allowed myself away from the prison underneath the Acosta pack house, I let my wolf free to walk the alleys, to traverse the greens, to breathe.

The cloak of early-morning darkness was all I really had going for me. I shouldn't have been out there. I shouldn't have been in wolf form, and I really shouldn't have left Fiona behind.

Over the last four months, I had softened toward her

a little bit. Maybe it was her easy acquiescence to my version of events with Wren. Maybe our conversations when the pair of us were far too bored for our own good bonded us a little bit.

Or maybe it was just that we were in prisons of our own making.

Four months of no running with my pack, no fresh air, no light, made me a little crazy. But more, it was because Fiona's time seemed to be running out. She couldn't stay under that null ward much longer.

I couldn't get her to eat.

I'd considered paying a doctor to put in a feeding tube or just shoving food down her throat. In the dark recesses of my mind—the ones I chose not to voice—I considered setting her free.

The ABI searched the city high and low for whoever had opened the gate. As far as I knew, they hadn't pinned it on anyone. That didn't mean Fiona was in the clear, but it did give me hope that on the off chance she *was* to go free, she might be safe. If it weren't for the boundary the ABI had put around the city as a whole, I would think it was a good idea.

Fiona's sanity had been slipping—bit by bit, day by day—and the longer she remained under those bars, the closer she got to wilting away to nothing. If we left her there, she'd end up starving to death.

If we set her free, the ABI could kill her.

I missed the days when I hated her. Missed the days when I didn't care if she lived or died. I longed for them more than I could possibly say. And so, I ran, pushing my wolf as far and as fast as he would go to run out this horrible burning in my gut and the worry that never seemed to go away.

I would have loved to know when the switch happened. I would have loved to know when I started giving a shit about a Jacobs witch. I'd love to know when I stopped caring who her father was and where she came from.

But I didn't know when I stopped seeing her as a Jacobs and started seeing her as only Fiona.

Somehow, by the time the sun really made an appearance, I'd directed my feet back to the pack house. Other than these last few years, I hadn't lived there in decades. When Wren was taken, I moved back home to help Nico be the Alpha we needed. But I missed being on my own, missed my home, my own furniture, my own things. I visited my estate occasionally—showering, changing, and then returning to the place where I'd grown up but never felt like home.

Every time I came down those steps after being away for even an hour, I feared I'd find her dead. This time, though, I could hear her breathing—the labor of her lungs making me want to scream.

I'd stopped being able to go in the cell with her weeks ago. There was a time in the early days when I could do things to make her more comfortable, and she would simply sleep through it. But now her sleep was fitful at best, constantly interrupted by either her hunger or the chill that never seemed to leave her bones.

It was like watching a car wreck in slow motion— when there was nothing you could do to stop it, but you couldn't tear your eyes away.

Fiona had tried to escape twice—not because her sane mind wanted to but when she lost herself to the hunger or the madness or the magic that I feared was still roiling beneath her skin. Both times she failed spectacularly—not even managing to exit the cell before her body had given out, and she wilted to the floor in a puddle of tears and gasping desperation.

This was the real punishment.

This was my penance for what I had done to Wren.

I had lost the woman who could have been my mate years ago, and yet I was not strong enough to fight my father's compulsion and put a knife to an innocent woman's neck. Fiona was in the cell for protection, not punishment. But I was watching over her because I deserved the slap in the face that watching her wilt most definitely was.

There wasn't a run I could take or vacation I could have that would remove the ache in my chest—nothing I could do that made watching Fiona slowly die any better. This was my penance—Nico's retribution for the wrong I'd done.

Fitting.

Gently, I lowered myself onto the metal folding chair. My siblings had tried to get me to move to something more comfortable, but I'd realized pretty early on that Fiona got the comfort. I didn't deserve it. Fiona had risked everything to get Wren back. She'd removed awful people from the world to gain power, and she opened the gate just like she said she would. Given what we now knew about the Prince of Hell, Zephyr, I had a feeling Wren's origins may have lent to the bastardization of that spell.

Fiona didn't deserve to be under these bars. But me? After all I had failed to do, and all I wished for? I knew that if she could stay breathing, I'd switch places with her in a heartbeat.

"Come on, Cupcake," I murmured, wishing I could open the door just once. "It's time to get up."

I wasn't quite sure when Fiona went from "Witch Bitch" to "Jacobs" to "Cupcake."

It was probably when we started trading favorite movies, foods, and colors. Fiona was the queen of a sudoku puzzle, and I could kick her ass every time at a game of *Clue*.

Somewhere in there, I started giving a shit about her.

Somewhere in there, I started caring whether she lived or died.

And there wasn't a second that went by where I didn't wish that I could forgive her family—that I could trust what I felt.

That I could believe she was safe.

Fiona's grunt was far less ladylike than she would have appreciated. As was the snuffling snort before her eyes peeled open, and she speared me with her baleful glare.

"I recall several discussions about you calling me that, Theo. Why must you annoy me?"

I held in a chuckle, the relief at her opening her eyes filling my bones. "We all need our kicks, Cupcake. Haven't you figured that out by now?"

Slowly, she sat up, her arms trembling as they barely shoved her vertical. "I'll remember that when it's my turn to annoy *you*."

"So I suppose you'll get your chance in about five minutes then."

She narrowed her eyes to slits. "Ha-ha. Very funny.

And why did you wake me up? I can't even sleep through my punishment anymore?"

It was a dick move to wake her up so early. She got so little sleep nowadays, but her breathing had scared the shit out of me. Each one was a congested whistle in her lungs. Nico would need to heal her again soon. That was if I could convince him to stop taking out his frustration on the arcane community.

"What, and you miss out on my sparkling personality? *Never.*"

On top of my worry about whether Fiona would live long enough to be free, I also worried a lot about my little brother. Nico hadn't taken the gate failure very well, and his despair was always on the edges of our pack bond underneath the danger that always seemed just around the corner.

"Come on, Cupcake. I'll let you try and beat me at *Clue* again. You're bound to win one of these days."

After three rounds of me summarily thrashing Fiona at *Clue*, I felt a shift in the air. One second, it was as if the weight of the world was on my shoulders, and the next, it was just gone. Joy filtered through the pack bond, but I didn't know if I could trust it.

Part of me dared to hope, and the other part knew it was too good to be true. Either way, there was no chance of me telling Fiona—not without knowing for sure.

"What is wrong with you?" she asked, moving my game piece to a room I'd cleared four times already. "Are you letting me win?"

Shaking myself, I eyed my note sheet. Truth be told, I already had the answer. It was Professor Plum, in the library, with the wrench. But I was too distracted by the unmitigated happiness seeping through the bond that I couldn't even think of a way to end the game.

"I'm fine," I snapped, my jaw clenching all on its very own. I was a liar. I doubted I'd been fine in the last three years.

Three years of waiting and watching my brother slowly lose his mind. How was I going to fix it if...

"Come on, something has to be up," Fiona insisted, her too-perceptive gaze boring a hole into the side of my cheek. She always did this. If I didn't know better, I would swear she still had magic—still could charm me into coughing up info. "Your face is doing that thing it does when it's worried, or it's a Tuesday, or you're constipated. I haven't really figured out exactly what all your expressions mean, but it's something. Do you need fiber?"

"I told you, I'm fine. Everything is fucking fine. Why do you have to do this?" I shoved myself to standing, looming over her like the asshole I was. "Every time. It's like you're trying to be annoying."

Fiona's brow went from furrowed in concern to completely smooth as if a mask was falling over her face. "Right. I think I'm done playing with you. I'm going to go do something else."

But she and I both knew there was nowhere for her to go. But even if she couldn't go anywhere physically, Fiona pretended like I wasn't even there.

It was for the best. I couldn't tell her what I thought it was. Hell, I didn't even want to admit it to myself.

What if I was wrong? What if I got her hopes up, and it all turned out to be a lie?

I was protecting her—if not from disappointment, then maybe from myself.

Fiona turned on the TV and did her level best to pick the most annoying movie known to mankind. The problem was, all the movies she thought I hated, I secretly kind of liked. The first of this marathon was *Practical Magic*. Little did she know, I always got choked up when Sally heard her daughters' cry for help, and she raced back to save them.

Unfortunately, the movie wasn't the only method of torture in Fiona's arsenal.

During the first movie, she went about giving herself a pedicure. That, I actually hated. It didn't matter how many candles we burned or how many air purifiers we had, the place was still a fucking dungeon, and the scent of nail lacquer was the bane of my existence.

Midway through the movie, I sensed a change come over the entire house. It had been buzzing for hours, the current of happiness filtering through us all. And though I could hear that my brother had returned, my ears still wouldn't let me believe the voice of the woman with him. It didn't matter if I couldn't see them, my ears picked up on so much on the floor above.

I sat in silence, gritting my teeth, and praying that I wasn't hallucinating.

8

THEO

An hour later, Fiona had moved on to *Legally Blonde.* Elle Woods was in the middle of the costume party debacle when three sets of footsteps thumped down the dungeon stairs.

A gust of relief fell from my lips as my brother and his wife moved into view. I hadn't been fooling myself. Wren really was back. Somehow, some way, she had waltzed back into Savannah after being gone for three years. With them was a giant, white wolf that rarely seemed to leave my brother's side.

Every member of the pack had a wolf inside them. Shifters were never just people who turned into wolves.

We were born with a wolf inside us, begging to get free. It was another consciousness, another entity. Honestly, sometimes it almost felt like being possessed. Because there were two minds in our heads at all times.

But the wolf at Nico's side wasn't like the rest of us.

Ghost used to belong to my father. And because my brother was an Alpha stronger than any I'd ever known, he could separate the man from the wolf. Before he'd taken our father's life, he ripped Ghost right out of him, the wolf no longer bound to the liminal cage of a shifter's human form.

And as much as I despised my father, his wolf was worse. That mangy fucking mutt pissed in my chair, tore up my shoes, and pretty much was a menace to society. It was the one perk of living down here. Ghost hated the dungeon. Personally, I'd rather have a Husky puppy than that fucking thing. Still, he was loyal to Nico, so I endured his existence until he proved otherwise.

Staring at the redhead at my brother's side, my jaw twitched, irrational anger filling my gut. All the work Fiona had done to get her back, and she just showed up out of the blue? I wanted answers, but asking for them was likely more than I deserved. The last time we'd been in the same room, I'd held a knife to her throat.

It didn't matter whether I hadn't been in control or not—I had still done her wrong.

Setting the book I'd been pretending to read on the floor, I stood, bowing my head as a sign of respect. "So, you're what all the commotion was about? I'm glad to see you made it home."

That was just as much a lie as it was the truth. A part of me resented the woman. The other part worried what seeing her would do to Fiona.

Wren tipped up her chin, ignoring me in earnest as she turned to the bars. "Hey, Troublemaker, I brought you some food."

I'd been so worried about Fiona that I hadn't even noticed the plate in her hands. Studying it, I picked apart the selections. Mashed potatoes were good, but Fiona didn't like gravy, even though she needed the calories. The meatloaf was always a good choice, but Fiona wouldn't eat it. She preferred fruit and raw veggies. Sometimes I could get her to drink one of those protein shakes humans gave to their underweight kids, but she wouldn't always finish them.

Fiona's multicolored braid whipped behind her back as she turned, her fragile body standing so fast, she immediately plopped back down. She put a trembling hand to her forehead, even as a wide smile flitted across her face.

"Did I fall off the deep end again, or am I finally dreaming in this gods-forsaken hellhole?"

Her eyes found mine, and I tried to relax my shoulders and jaw, making my face a blank mask so she wouldn't worry. "If you're hallucinating, Cupcake, then so am I."

I almost breathed a sigh of relief at her scalding glare. *Almost.*

That right there was why I hadn't told her—well, that, and the fact that Wren didn't come down here right away. There was a decent amount of resentment for that as well churning in my gut.

"I leave for three measly years, and the world falls apart," Wren joked, shaking her head, pasting a broad smile on her face. "Now, I know for a fact these mashed potatoes and gravy are the best I've ever tasted, so you really need to get them while they're hot."

Fiona's eyes misted up, and I wanted to hug her and punch my brother in the face. This was going to set her back, I just knew it. "It's really you? You're really here?"

But all I could do was watch as Fiona was built up only to be knocked down.

Helpless. The word you're looking for is helpless.

Wren's bottom lip trembled. "In the flesh."

What gall she had to cry. Fiona hated tears. She wouldn't even let them fall during the saddest movies, and trust me, she'd made it through *A Dog's Purpose* dry-eyed. Even I couldn't do that.

But Fiona sucked in a huge breath as tears spilled down her cheeks.

Tears.

I was going to fucking murder someone.

"I'm not dreaming?" she whispered, looking from Wren to me to Nico and then back to me.

Her looking to me to confirm it loosened the knot in my gut a bit, but I still wanted to punch someone.

Wren's smile wobbled as she got closer to the bars. "If you need me to pinch you, I can do that, but I'd rather you just take my word for it. Now let me in there so I can hug the shit out of you."

Oh, fuck no.

Wren moved to open the door, but I stood right in her way. No way was she going to get Fiona killed just because she was back, and it didn't matter if she was mad —which the woman clearly was—there was no way in hell I was going to let her put Fiona in danger, I didn't give a shit if she was Wren's best friend.

"I can't let you do that."

Her eye actually twitched as Nico's growl erupted through the dungeon.

Perfect. Just what I needed. An execution to go along with the shame. Just what I always wanted.

But instead of my brother taking me to task, I got a pissy redhead with her hands on her hips. "How about you don't *let* me do a gods-damned thing, and you get the fuck out of my way, Theo?"

Here we go.

"Look, I get it. I fucked up." Okay, that was a shitty effort as far as apologies went, but there were only so many times I could say sorry for shit I had no control over.

And my half-assed sorry went over about as well as a lead balloon.

"I'm going to need more than an 'I fucked up.' I'm going to need a damn good reason to not put a knife to *your* throat," she hissed, her eyes flashing the same gold that Nico's did when he was pissed, "make *you* bleed, to make *your* family watch as some bitch damn near cuts your head off. I don't know what you said to Nico to make him forgive your sorry ass, but I'm not him. I'm going to need an actual apology, or so help me, I will rip your insides out and wear your hollowed-out carcass as a motherfucking party dress."

There was a hardness to Wren that hadn't been there three years ago. It made me believe every word out of her mouth. "That was... graphic."

She leveled me with a scalding glare. "And also, one hundred percent true."

If I'd been in wolf form, I had a feeling I'd be showing

her my belly. "Look, I would love to say I'm sorry and explain and have everything be peaches and fucking cream, all right?" Rubbing the back of my neck, my shoulders climbed toward my ears. "But the truth is, until you have your will taken away from you, you can never understand. I didn't want to hurt you. I would never hurt someone's mate. I just co—"

"Stop," she ordered, pulling me up short. "Your father?" she suggested, right on the money.

I nodded, bowing my head further, nearly bending in half. Following his orders—whether I had a choice or not—was my greatest shame. I'd nearly taken my brother's mate from him. I'd almost damned him to the same sorry existence I had. I'd nearly...

"I'm sorry, Wren. I didn't want to hurt you. None of us did. Well, maybe Santi, but he's come around since you saw him last."

Grumbling, she crossed her arms. "Forgiven," she huffed, almost like it was being pulled from her kicking and screaming. "Though, you still need to get out of my way."

I winced, not budging an inch. "I—"

"I swear to everything holy," Wren snarled through gritted teeth, "if the word 'let' comes out of your mouth, we're going to have a problem."

We already had a problem—she just didn't know it yet.

"Look," I barked, glancing over my shoulder for a second to meet Fiona's gaze. Her expression was a mix of betrayed and resigned, and it killed me to have to say this. Dropping my voice to a whisper, I turned back to Wren. "You can't go in there. It took ages to get this set up going, and you being here will probably disrupt everything we've built. If you go in there, she's going to want to get out. And if Fiona leaves that cell, the ABI will be on her ass in a heartbeat."

Confusion pulled at her brow as she looked between Nico and me. "What? You planning on leaving her in there forever?"

I straightened, my jaw practically turning to stone. The part of me that blamed Wren for all of this reared its ugly head. "No, I don't plan on imprisoning your friend until the end of time. Just until we figure out how to close the gate to Hell she accidentally opened trying to get your ass from the fucking Fae realm."

Wren stumbled back a step, her gaze flitting to each of us before her legs almost buckled. "I'm sorry, *what*?"

Had Nico told her nothing? She'd been back all damn day. Had he just skipped the part where the city was on literal fire?

"Someone needs to tell me what the fuck is going on, and someone needs to do it right now."

Nico's arm wrapped around her middle, his voice low and calm. "It's my fault. Fiona was just trying to—"

"Oh, for fuck's sake," Fiona shouted, drawing all our attention. "The only one to blame is me. It was me and my fool hubris and my need to be right. Had I listened to that Fae fucker just once, I wouldn't be in this mess, but here we are."

She approached the bars, her steps shaky and stilted. They faltered a bit, but she didn't dare touch the metal. "But if what I did means that you're really here and I haven't gone off my nut again, well, I'll take it."

I snatched the plate out of Wren's hands, fitting it into a little metal slot in the cell door. "Eat something." At her raised eyebrow, I tacked on a begrudging, "Please."

She took the foil-covered plate and the bundle of utensils and sat on the cold floor, not bothering to unwrap either, even though she had to be starving. "I was the one who messed up. I thought your blood would make it a snap to open the Fae gates, and boy, did that come to bite me in the ass. Though, thinking it through, the one we should really be blaming is Margot. Had I known your origins, I would have crafted my spell a little better."

Ah, yes. Wren Bannister was kin to a Prince of Hell.

Had she let that little tidbit slip, we would all be in a very different place. Exactly *how* Wren was related to Zephyr was a mystery, but I had a feeling we were about to find out.

"You mean my little jaunt to the Fae realm as a child, or the stars I was born under because the Seelie Queen talked about th—"

"Jaunt to the Fae realm?" I growled. No one said anything at all about a field trip to the Fae realm.

Rolling her eyes, Wren sat on the floor, and Ghost parked his big ass right next to her hip, half-laying, half-sitting on her like a real dog. She scratched him right behind his ears, his giant head resting on her knee.

It was all real fucking cozy except for the bombshell she'd just dropped.

"Evidently, this last one was not my first visit. When I was a kid, my parents always talked about 'the incident' that had me transferring to a human school. No one said dick about it being me opening a Fae door and just waltzing right through into the Seelie Queen's throne room. By the time I made it back, they'd just assumed I was dead and moved on with their lives."

And yeah, none of us knew about that, but... Did that mean Wren *didn't* know about Zephyr? Nico and I traded wide eyes over Wren's head, the expression on his face telling me he was thinking the same damn thing as I was.

"Why do I get the feeling I'm not going to like what you're about to tell me?"

Fiona winced, fiddling with the napkin around her utensils while Nico and I shrugged at each other. Luckily, Fiona wasn't a coward like the two of us.

"After you were taken, that Fae fucker locked down all the doors to the realm. No one could get in or out, meaning you couldn't get out even if you tried. But he disappeared, and we had to find him."

It had taken six months. Six months of hunting down leads, of calling in favors. And I almost missed those days to the ones we were in now.

"The first order of business," she continued, "was finding the illusion mage who made the deal with him to get his daughter back. And after we had his name, we could summon him. Unfortunately, I didn't have enough power to summon him on my own—not for months. We called in favors, made deals, did everything we could just to get him." She shook her head, her shoulders drooping. "But when we got him, he wouldn't talk. Wouldn't do anything but sit there and wait us out. So, I... got creative."

Fiona hugged her legs to her chest as if she were freezing, and I had the strongest urge to rip the door off its hinges and put a blanket around her shoulders.

"If I didn't have the power to open the door myself,

and if Nico couldn't break him, and if that pixie dust motherfucker wouldn't do what was right, then I thought I could borrow his power and do it, anyway. And it worked—*sort of*. I opened a door all right. I just opened the wrong fucking one."

Silence reigned for a long, pregnant pause before something like understanding dawned on Wren's face.

"Okay, but the door you opened in Chatham Square?" Wren clarified to Fiona's reluctant nod. "Is the one I came through, so you didn't open the wrong one. You made it so I could come home. But I'm fuzzy on why my origins make a difference or why the city is on literal fire."

Wren hadn't connected the dots, and as much as I resented her witchy ass, I so did not want to be the one to tell her.

"Because she didn't open a door to the Fae realm," Nico answered, kneeling at his wife's side. "She opened a door to Hell. That's why there are demons all over Savannah. It's why the ABI is trying their best to contain the city. Why if they ever figure out Fiona is the source of the power that opened it, she isn't just going to be on house arrest. She'll be dead."

I plopped back onto my folding chair, irritated he was missing the best part. "You skipped the part about

Zephyr. I really want to see her face when you tell her she's kin to a Prince of Hell."

Well, if he wouldn't do it...

"Excuse me?" Wren squeaked, making my sadistic little heart sing.

"Way to go, dipshit," Fiona grumbled, watching Wren's face like a hawk.

I couldn't help it. It was too good an opportunity to pass up.

Nico stood, smacked me upside the head, and then continued his crouch by his wife's side. "When Fiona opened the gate, a demon walked out of it. A Prince of Hell."

Wren looked like she was about to throw up. If I wasn't so worried about what she'd do to get Fiona out of that cell, I would have laughed.

"He claims he is your kin, but in demon-speak that could mean anything. He's been reluctant to spill the details, only that when you came home, he would like to meet you."

That was more than I knew. *Damn Nico and his fucking secrets.* When exactly had he been meeting with the prince?

And then, as if my thoughts and our conversation summoned him, because one moment, there were just the four of us and Ghost in this dungeon, and the next, there was a giant, redheaded demon sitting on a leather wingback. It was as if he'd been there the whole time, his curled black horns reaching for the ceiling as he inspected Nico's wife like she was the answer to everything.

And that's when I knew we were well and truly *fucked*.

9

FIONA

The last time I'd been in the presence of the Prince of Hell, I'd passed out. Now that I wasn't consumed by dark magic, well...

It was entirely possible I was going to wilt like a damn flower. The last four months had done a number on me, but I was almost positive that what I was seeing was actually real. Considering everyone stared at the same damn thing I was, I figured I wasn't hallucinating.

"Hello, Zephyr," Nico called, scooting Wren behind him like he had a chance in hell of protecting her against a literal demon. "How can I help you?"

Zephyr tilted his head to the side, peering around Nico to his wife. "You can stop hiding my kin, Alpha. She is in no danger from me. In fact, I aim to save her from those who would do her harm."

"Sweet Mary, please tell me this dude is not my dad," Wren griped, getting to her feet. She skirted around Nico and Ghost's giant wolf body, getting closer to her *kin*. "No offense to you, but my mother is already Satan's mistress. I do not need an actual demon as my sperm donor. And if you are actually my dad, I'm going to need you to lie to me on this one."

Zephyr's face split into a wide grin, his gaze softening as he stared at Wren. "I do not need to lie. I would never lay with a woman like Margot Bannister. No offense to you, but I have met Eldritch demons with more soul than that woman."

Wren tried to cover her mouth, but the laugh still echoed through the dungeon like the half-crazed witch cackle it was. "So, you're acquainted."

I'd gotten the gist when it came to Wren and her family. Hers made mine look like the fucking Waltons or something. Personally, I preferred *the Addams Family*, but *damn*. I had been used and manipulated, but I couldn't say my father ever used me like his own personal battery pack and drained me dry.

"Quite. And I will say the entire Bannister line is something of a case study in Hell. They use them to teach the young demons how to be petty."

I let out a derisive snort. *I fucking bet they do. They probably have Jacobs' ones down there to teach them how to be evil, too.*

Zephyr's gaze fell on me like he'd heard my thoughts and agreed. Then he studied the cage I was in. Truth be told, it was some of my finer work. Too bad I couldn't get out of the damn thing. As much relief as I felt to have Wren back—to have actually done something, anything, to have aided her return—I really wanted out of this cell.

"But the real question is why you have caged the witch? Did she do something she shouldn't?" He tilted his head to the side before snapping his fingers, the bars to my cell melting away to nothing. "That's better."

My gut bottomed out as the first bit of relief warred with a boatload of worry. It was as if someone had stolen a security blanket—if that blanket was made of fucking concrete. The weight was gone, the churning bile in my gut, the ache in my bones, but also, so was the safety.

"What the fuck do you think you're doing?" Theo growled, putting himself between Zephyr and me.

Hell, he did one better and snatched me right up off the floor like I weighed nothing and herded me behind him like he thought the demon would attack at any moment. "She needs that cage so the ABI doesn't cut her fucking head off, you asshole. Put it back."

Zephyr's growl nearly made me pass out. I couldn't

see him past Theo's giant back, but the sound of his censure was enough to chill my bones. "You're the one who stuck her in a cage," he accused, the pitch deepening with each word. "Did you not realize you were killing her? Little by little every day, she was dying. And now she is not. Maybe now she can eat without vomiting it all back up five minutes later."

Theo's head whipped to me, his accusatory glare making me feel about four inches tall. I figured he knew I couldn't keep anything down, but he wasn't as much in the know as I'd thought. And we both knew I was dying —one way or another. But Theo's grip was strong as iron but so gentle it was as if he thought I would break at any second.

I had been dying. If it wasn't the bars themselves, it was the black magic in me poisoning me still—not that I'd tell them that.

"You were right to want her out from behind those bars," Zephyr pressed, his conversation carrying on with Wren as if Theo and I weren't having the mother of all stare-downs three paces away. "Your instincts will hone with time, but you need to listen to your gut more. Don't let that dreadful woman's voice ring in your head. Yes?"

They continued on, but Theo didn't so much as blink as what might be fear bloomed all over his face. And for some reason, I couldn't make myself look away, couldn't tear my eyes from his, couldn't breathe.

"Speaking of your mother," Zephyr commented, snapping his fingers just like he'd done before stealing me from under the bars. A moment later, it felt as if someone had taken a hook to my middle, yanking me through space and time and dumping us all in the parlor of a stuffy house that had seen better days.

Wren scrambled back, eyes wide as her breaths sawed in and out of her lungs. "Why would you bring me here?" she hissed, her gaze darting to every corner of the room like she'd get attacked at any minute.

I had no idea where we were, but I had a feeling it wasn't good.

"Don't worry, youngling. There is nothing to fear from this place anymore," Zephyr practically cooed, standing from his makeshift throne, and then I knew.

This was Wren's family home, and he'd brought her back—brought us all back where we most definitely should *not* be.

Ghost didn't like it at all. He braced himself between the four of us and the demon like he was seriously considering taking a chunk out of him.

"Yeah, right," Wren scoffed, her anger getting the better of her. "You know nothing of what these people put me through."

Zephyr's scales rippled, indicating that the demon was not happy with how this conversation was going. "I have an idea. And since it is my fault, I am here to make it right."

"Your fault?"

Zephyr sighed before turning, his giant hand gesturing to us to follow. "If you want the story, you're going to have to trust me just a little. Follow me."

Wren and Nico exchanged an uncertain glance before her face blanked. She firmed her jaw and gave him a jerky nod. Once again, Wren was going to put on a brave face when she should have run screaming in the other direction.

I stepped around Theo, but his grip—which had never left me—yanked me back. It might have been gentle, but it pissed me off all the same.

"I don't think so, Cupcake. The ABI will be here any second. I—"

At another snap of Zephyr's fingers, Theo let my wrist go and began following Zephyr like a mindless automaton.

Oh, hell no. You let him go right now.

No one took Theo's choices away from him. No one. Not after what his father had done to him.

Nico and I shared the sentiment because his growl

was long and low, making all of us freeze. "Let him go. No one takes his will away. Not *ever* on my watch."

Zephyr sighed. "This is not going how I planned at all." He snapped his fingers once more, giving Theo control of his body again before turning to me. "The ABI isn't looking for you, Fiona. They believe the Bannister family were the ones to open the portal. There is no need to hide. You're *welcome*. Now"—He paused, eyeing Theo like he'd really enjoy squishing him underneath his big leather boot—"do you want answers, or do you want to stay in the dark?"

Steeling my back, I swallowed hard even though it hurt. Taking away those bars didn't do a damn thing to heal me. I'd been under those fucking things for months, but I wouldn't let my poor bones fail me—not ever.

"Oh, you bet your ass I'm coming."

But Wren stood in front of me, holding out her hand like she wanted me to take it. Reluctantly, I did, and it was as if I'd touched a live wire. More energy than I'd ever felt filled my bones as all the aches and pains melted away. Nico might have tried to heal me once or twice, but Wren? With power like that, it was no wonder a Fae King had been on her ass, or his son would close every gate there was.

Power-hungry men did awful things when they thought no one was looking. I knew from experience.

Wren let my hand go to wipe her nose, her fingers coming away red, and my heart shriveled in my chest. She'd used too much of her power, and now she was bleeding.

For me.

All I'd tried to do for her, and she gave away her power so freely—even to her detriment. It didn't matter how bad off I was, I couldn't let her do that again.

"You planning on teaching her how to combat that little hurdle?" Nico barked, cradling his wife to his chest, and I had to agree.

Three years ago, Wren didn't have that first clue how to use magic, and if she was going to do it now, she needed someone to teach her how.

"You aren't drawing on the earth like you should. Or the ether," Zephyr scolded. "You are breaking your own body down to give it away, and while I appreciate the sentiment, you need to stop."

Wren gnashed her teeth, pushing out of Nico's arms. "You and that damn Seelie Queen keep saying the same thing, but you don't explain it, you don't tell me what that means. Draw from nothing, from liminal spaces, draw from fucking what? It makes no sense."

The prince studied her a bit. "Did they teach you nothing?"

And damn if I didn't agree with him. She was part of

one of the oldest witch families in existence, and she knew nothing about what it was to be a witch.

Wren's eyes started glowing. "Why would they teach me anything? I was their battery, not their equal. I was the fuel for their spells, not their family, not their blood. You call me your kin, but what exactly am I to you? I'm not your daughter, not your cousin, not your anything. I didn't see you waltzing in here when my mother locked me in a fucking closet for spilling a glass of chocolate milk. I was five. You know how long I was in that closet? Two days. Covered in vomit and piss and shit because I was so scared."

Her palm lit, something she had never done in my presence. Theo yanked me away, his eyes as big as saucers as she continued to rant. She pointed to the closet in question, and I knew then what I'd done to open the gate hadn't been enough.

I should have found her family.

I should have picked them off one by one.

I should have watched them suffer like they deserved.

It didn't matter that I'd taken out some of the worst witches in Savannah. I hadn't killed *the* worst.

"Where the fuck were you when she didn't speak to me for a month after I accidentally set the lawn on fire because she did a spell too close to me? Do you know what that does to a child? No one would speak to me—

not my parents, not my aunts or cousins, not my grandmother. I was seven. No 'I love you,' no 'good night,' not one word. Eventually, I stopped talking, too. I brought home straight A's, and it didn't matter. I broke things. I begged. Nothing mattered. She didn't talk until I was good enough for long enough. If it weren't for Ellie and Alice, I would have gone insane. If I'm your kin, where the fuck were you?"

I'd been in the exact same position as she had—begging for a kind word from family that never seemed to... never... It was no wonder we'd bonded in ABI school. No wonder we'd been thick as thieves since day one.

And I'd be damned if her family ever touched her again.

Nico murmured into her ear, and a moment later, the flame in her palm went out.

Zephyr's face split into a smile. "Control. You've learned it so quickly. I'm impressed."

"I don't give a shit if you're impressed. I care about knowing who and what I am and learning to master whatever power I've got. Can you do that, or are you going to leave me to the wolves?"

He considered her, his black eyes calculating as they looked her over. "Fair enough. Follow me."

Zephyr led us through Wren's childhood home. At

one time it must have been beautiful. The dark mahogany floors, expensive sconces, and plush carpets had all seen better days. Dust coated everything along with a heavy layer of debris. Broken bottles and food wrappers, and pages from grimoires littered the ground.

Someone was living here—had to be.

"They thought their wards were good enough, but hubris will get people like that every time." He snapped his fingers, revealing a hidden door in one of the beaten-up wooden panels.

Theo covered his nose, and a moment later, I did the very same. Something had died behind that door, and he wanted us to follow him? Unless the Bannister family was in a decaying heap, I wanted no part of it. It seemed my former jailer was of the same mind because he tucked me behind him and moved us backward.

"Please tell me there is a point to this," Nico growled, clutching Wren to his back as he mimicked us, moving away from the door of death.

Zephyr's smile would haunt me until the day I died. "It is her revenge. Would you deny her that?"

Revenge?

Well, I could work with that.

10

THEO

"I don't need revenge," Wren whispered, and it was as if she'd taken away Christmas, told me the Tooth Fairy was a lie, and snaked the damn Easter Bunny out from under me.

Revenge was my favorite—especially when it involved the Bannister Coven—and she was about to cancel it.

"The fuck you don't," Fiona hissed, shaking her wrist from my hold and damn near shoving me out of the way. I would have objected, but the little jerk took the words right out of my mouth.

"I showed you basic kindness, and you acted like I was giving you the most precious gift," Fiona ranted, her whole body vibrating with righteous indignation. "I treated you like a person, and it was as if you'd only gotten that round about never in your life. Day in and day out for how many years have you been alive now?"

My gut bottomed out, and the words Wren had said when we first met made a whole lot more sense. I'd been an asshole to her, trying to rile her on purpose to see what the bond was really like between her and Nico. My brother's wife—his mate—refused to be intimidated. But with this new knowledge, I knew I was child's play compared to the abuse she'd suffered.

Wren waggled her hand. "Twenty-four-ish years, but I don't know the date anymore. I could be twenty-eight by now."

Fiona planted her fists on her hips, stomping her foot. "Not the fucking point, and you know it. Stop changing the subject. And if you won't do it for revenge, do it for me. Those bitches need to take the fall for the Hell gate fiasco, and dead bitches are much easier to pin shit on than live ones."

If anyone knew how to get out of bullshit, it would be Fiona. Given who her daddy was, I was surprised she hadn't offered this option already.

"*Fine*. There better be nose bleach after this," Wren grumbled before tipping her chin at Zephyr to lead the way.

Zephyr ducked, his horns nearly scraping the stone ceiling as he moved down the stairs. Reluctantly, we followed Nico, the scent of the dungeon invading my nose as we took hesitant steps on the slick stone. I had to catch Fiona three times so she didn't slip and take us all down with her. Still, despite our less-than-stealthy descent into a pit of near-total darkness, there was not so much as a whisper in greeting.

Way too good to be true.

There was no way the Bannister house wouldn't be warded out the ass. Knowing that family, there should be sigils on every bit of stone and every wooden support. It should have been completely covered. It should have smelled like ozone and spent magic, but all I smelled was death.

A lot of it.

"I don't like this. This isn't right," Wren hissed at Nico's back, and I couldn't help but agree with her. "No wards, no protection? This is fucked."

At the base of the stairs were three curved paths cut from a rough rock wall, the cave of a dungeon branching out into what seemed like nothingness. But it wasn't until we reached the antechamber right before the paths, did shit really go sideways.

Fiona—the only one who couldn't see in the dark— snapped her fingers, using her magic for the first time in months. A pretty pink flame bloomed in her hand like a rose, and I saw her face soften in joy for one single, solitary moment before spells came at us from all sides.

Just like I'd done all damn day, I snatched Fiona off her feet, ducking back into the stairwell. I covered her with my body, shielding her from harm. Orbs of magic exploded against the stone, but I couldn't think about that. Oh, no, I was too busy holding onto a hellcat trying to get back into the fray.

"They need help," Fiona pleaded, shoving at my shoulders with her magic. "It's my fault, you have to let me—"

"I don't have to let you do shit," I growled, shoving her back until I was sure no spells could hit her. "Knock it off, Cupcake, or else I'll put you over my shoulder and fucking make you."

I should have gone back—should have helped my Alpha. Should have at least helped Wren. But something kept me rooted to the spot. Something made me stay with Fiona. And no, I had no intention of examining just why that was.

Nico let out a moan of pain, and I had to make myself turn back to the action, the worry for my little brother warring with my need to keep Fiona out of it. An orb of electricity slammed into Nico, knocking him into the stone wall, and I moved.

I was just about to yank him out of the melee when Wren began to glow like the damn sun. Every spell and orb of magic flew to her and her alone as if she were summoning them, but they didn't hit her exactly.

No, they melted into her, making her glow brighter, hotter, like she was absorbing the magic somehow. An orb she missed hit Ghost, another hit Nico, burning them both. Nico let out a pained grunt, Ghost whined, and Wren let out an unholy scream.

All the hairs on my arms and neck stood up as Wren detonated. Rivers of fire flew from her hands, snaking down the three darkened paths like a tidal wave of fire, the blaze coating everything. No one—no spell, no witch, no arcaner whatsoever was surviving that unless they were gods-damned fireproof.

Slowly, the flames petered out, and Wren was left a shaky mess on her hands and knees. I could have sworn she'd said all those years ago that she couldn't do magic. I didn't know what that was, but it sure as shit looked like a fuck-load of magic to me.

Zephyr's paw of a hand hauled Wren to her feet, but she batted him away in favor of stumbling toward my brother.

"Jesus, fuck, Bird," he rumbled, getting to his feet, his arms closing around her like she was the most precious thing in the universe.

I wanted to thump him on the head. I had done the right thing and got my—*Fiona*—out of there. He had just stood there like an idiot while his wife did all the work. *Moron.*

"Are you hurt? Is Ghost okay? I need a nap, I think. I'm tired."

Nico lifted her into his arms, snarling at Zephyr when he tried to touch her. "This is your fucking fault. Bringing her here—letting them hurt her again—this is your doing, and I swear if she—"

"I'm fine," she whispered, patting his chest with a weak hand, and I was right back in my father's office all those years ago, watching their bond bloom bright—learning that I had been deceived by my father, that he'd lied and coerced and forced all our hands to do something evil.

Shame filled my gut, and I dropped my gaze to the dirty stone floor.

"Sweet Pea, your ears are bleeding," Fiona sassed from behind me, nearly knocking me over as she elbowed me out of her way. "If you'd admit you're a little more than not fine, that would be awesome. No offense, but this stoic, Alpha's wife bullshit is already getting old."

Ain't that the fucking truth.

"I just need a nap," Wren mumbled, and that's when I lost it.

"You need a fucking keeper," I grumbled. "You two ever heard of ducking and letting the giant demon prince handle shit? I thought you were supposed to be her mate not her charge, little brother."

Nico hugged his wife to his chest. "Fuck you, Theo."

Didn't he know how lucky he was? Didn't he know— "Yeah, yeah. Fuck me, and you're the one who let her stand there and—"

Wren peeled open an eyelid, her sclera bloodshot and her pupils blown wide. "Fuck you, Theo."

Ghost poked his wet nose in her cheek, eyeing Zephyr's approach. The demon was exasperated, just like the rest of us.

"I stand corrected. You do not have even the smallest inkling of control. You do, however, have an anger problem and the power to strip an entire compound of magic, so, well done there. Here," he said on a sigh, pressing the pad of his finger against her forehead. "This should fix it."

A moment later, Wren thrashed like she was being electrocuted. If it wasn't for the blood drying before my very eyes, I would have tackled the fucker. Wren bolted out of Nico's arms, her palms lighting with fire.

"Someone is down here. Two... no, three."

"Yes, well," Zephyr murmured, snapping his fingers.

As if pulled by a string, three women flew from their paths, colliding in a heap at Zephyr's feet. Another snap later, a black ring encircled them before glowing red with an unspent fire.

Eloise, Margot, and Judith Bannister.

Those three women had been a bane to the city of Savannah as a whole. They'd lorded power, hoarded it, and used it to get whatever they wanted under the guise of witch civility.

"That's enough spells from you three," the demon quipped, his smile wide. "Wren, my dear, say hello to the last three Bannister witches on the planet."

She opened her mouth to correct him—likely to include herself—but he held up a finger.

"You are not a Bannister witch. As someone who has never been inducted into their coven, any claim you have to that name ended when you married into the Acosta pack. Therefore, any curses, spells, or debts—soul or otherwise—of the Bannister name do not affect you."

Eloise shoved away from her daughters, climbing to her feet as if all three hundred years had finally caught up with her. My mother was older than the coven matriarch by about a decade, and yet, it was as if time had not been kind to the old hag.

"Well, if it isn't the screw-up and her mongrel,"

Wren's grandmother spat. "What? You come to finish us off, you ungrateful little bitch?"

Nico's growl vibrated through the dungeon, and I had to hold Fiona back from hauling across the room and slapping someone. The little spitfire didn't need to get in the middle of this.

But Wren had a lot of people in her corner, and Nico wasn't having it. "You'd better think up a spell to shut them up, demon, or else they won't live long enough to play out whatever bullshit scenario you brought us here for. They insult my wife again, and I'm ripping their tongues from their heads. You understand me?"

Zephyr's smile was practically beatific. "I like you. You're a good husband and protector. I approve." His attention shifted to Eloise. "Your input is no longer needed. You may stay silent now."

Ghost circled the spelled ring, his growl growing louder by the second while the three women remained silent.

"Now, I brought you here so you could have your mother tell you how you came to be, but seeing how they treat you, I'm not sure this was a good idea," Zephyr mused, tapping his chin.

I threw up my hands, finally letting go of the hellcat trying to plot revenge. "Ya *think*?" I growled, looking at the demon like he was a complete moron. "Perhaps you should ask people before you transport them places and make them relive childhood trauma, maybe? Fuck, man, are you *new* or something?"

Wren snort-laughed, but I was just done. Nico had been injured in the middle of this. My pack could be without an Alpha because he wanted some fucked up arcane version of a *Maury* episode. He put everyone in the room in danger because he didn't fucking think. As the reigning king of the same damn thing, I could call a spade a spade.

"I should have kept you mindless, wolf. Your mouth is going to get you into trouble one day."

"That's what they tell me." My smile was little better than a sneer as I threw my arms wide. "And yet, I'm still here."

"Can we get back on task, please?" Wren griped. "How I came to be? The whole sordid tale—can we get back to that before I get the black plague from this dank-ass dungeon?"

Zephyr sniffed, his eyebrow raising in indignation before he snapped his fingers. "Margot, why don't you tell us all about the deal you made?"

He said it like a request, but it was a command if I ever heard one.

Margot's eyes narrowed to slits as she stood like she

was gearing up to spew enough vitriol to power a small country.

"Why else would I summon a demon? Power. Had I known what I do now, I would have never done it. You failed to hold up your end of the bargain."

Zephyr stood to his full height. "I fulfilled every aspect of our deal. It was you who failed to be clear. You asked for power, and I gave it to you. It's not my fault you lost it. You asked for wealth and influence, and had you actually fostered any kind of goodwill, you would have had it for the rest of your days. Instead, you ostracized the one person who could have given you everything you asked for and more."

Margot's evil smile grew wide as she stared at her daughter like she was shit on her shoe. "You, my *darling* daughter, are what happens when a demon deal goes south while pregnant."

My sister-in-law was part demon?

Fantastic.

FIONA

Even though Margot's revelation should have been a bombshell, that didn't seem like the most pertinent thing to point out.

Her stupidity was.

"Who the fuck makes a demon deal while pregnant?" I'd heard of some stupid shit in my time, but as far as demon deals went, that was up there on the list of "what not to do." I stared at Margot like she was three sandwiches shy of a full lunch.

Margot's gaze sliced to me, and it might have been intimidating at some point, but it just wasn't right then. "It wasn't like I knew, okay? I was only six weeks along.

How was I supposed to know that her father's sperm were impervious to every birth control spell in the book?"

Too. Much. Information.

"That…" Wren began, her face a little green, "actually makes me hate you a little less, and I didn't think that was possible." She was on her own on that one. "But a demon deal for power? Even I'm not that stupid, and I've done some questionable shit in my day."

Judith stood, her calculating expression the most malicious out of the group. "Yes, we all know about your penchant for *missteps*."

Margot flipped her matted red curls from her shoulder. "There was no way around it. The Acosta pack was expanding, the Fae wanted payment, and there were some upstart covens trying to take what our family fought and died for. Power was the only way."

Judith snorted. "It should have been me. If we had gone with the plan as I laid it out, none of this would be happening, and yo—"

Eloise's hand cracked against her youngest daughter's face. "It was your thirst for blood that got us in this situation in the first place. You killed that Fae child for spell ingredients. What did you think would happen?"

"Does anyone else have a hankering for popcorn?" Theo mused, massaging his temples like the Bannisters were giving him a migraine. "Because I know telenovelas with less drama. *Shit.*"

"Does any of this have a point?" Wren barked, eyeing her family like the scum they were.

"It does. You see, Margot made a deal for power, but since her soul is just as black as her sister's, I couldn't in good conscience give it to her directly. Tell me—have you ever played Corrupt a Wish?"

Zephyr went on, explaining Wren's origins, how he gave her the power, how he made it so Margot never really had it. But I had no idea how someone could be so stupid. Even tangentially, giving the Bannisters power was akin to arming a nuclear warhead.

"To stop them from what?" Wren growled, her eyes glowing bright as she turned on the demon. "Cursing me to drain the power you gave me? The power she was promised? Not for nothing, but do you happen to think about the consequences of your actions, or are you a 'fly by the seat of your pants' kind of demon?"

She wasn't wrong.

"And you three," she hissed, turning back to her family. "All your scheming, all your talk of power, and what do you have? Dirty clothes and janky hair, and a gods-damned dungeon in the middle of an apocalypse you probably had a hand in creating. I swear, for all the times you called me a fuck-up, I would like you to look around at your current circumstances and eat your fucking words."

"That's rich," Judith hissed. "You couldn't even break my wards with all your *power*, but sure, you're not a fuck-up. A waste is more like it."

Zephyr stepped in between them, staring down at Judith like he would really enjoy burning the flesh from her bones. "And how many sacrifices did you make to strengthen that ward, witch?"

One thing about Judith, she had a spine made of steel. "Evidently not enough since she's still alive, but don't you worry. I'll be sure to do better next time."

"I thought we discussed this," Nico growled, pulling Wren away from the circle. "Either end them, or I will."

Sighing, Wren tugged Nico away, trying to head back for the stairs. "I'd like to leave. If you're done with this walk down memory lane, I have about a million places I would rather be."

"I am not done with you, child," Zephyr growled, snapping his fingers. "It is time for your revenge."

That snapping sound was compounded by the ward surrounding the remains of Wren's family breaking.

Oh, fuck.

Margot shot a spell across the now-open space, aiming right for Wren faster than a lightning strike. Smartly, both Nico and Wren ducked, and before Theo could jump into the fray or Ghost could take a chunk out of someone, Wren took over. Just like before, she began to glow, drawing the magic from the air, stealing the power from her family like she was a magnet.

But it was different. Stock-still, I stood, watching as my best friend siphoned the magic right out of their bones—it was so similar to how I'd stolen the magic from the witches to open the gate that it made my gut churn.

I wanted to scream, wanted to cry, but all I could do was let her do it.

Because they didn't deserve to be witches. They'd exploited every facet of their power for their own gain. They'd murdered their own family, their own blood, and for what? To hide in a dungeon until the world ended?

"This is what you deserve," Wren hissed, drawing their power away from them in large golden streams. "To have human years and human lives and human protection—which is none, in case you were wondering. You get human health and human fragility. And when you are old and decrepit and begging for death, I want you to remember me. You don't get to just shuffle off this mortal coil. No, death is too good for you. You get to *live*."

Granted, in the middle of the mess of Savannah, their lives would be mighty short, but it would be enough to get the point across.

The three women crumpled at her feet, but even as

much as they'd hurt her, Wren wouldn't kill them. My gaze tracked to Theo, his jaw like granite as he shook his head.

This was a very bad idea. It was the worst idea in the history of time.

"Are you sure, child?" Zephyr asked, assessing her with an inscrutable expression. "Are you positive you want them to live?"

You know better. They'll find a way to kill her before they take their last breath. Don't let her do this.

Zephyr raised an eyebrow, so I knew that fucker heard me, but he ignored me all the same.

"Are you asking me if I want their blood on my hands?" Wren griped. "Because if so, the answer is no. They cursed me so magic was lost to me. They took more than their fair share. What do you do to a bully who takes and takes and takes? You cut them off so they can't take more. This is enough."

It wasn't enough—it would probably never be enough.

"And what if I told you that the reason they are the last Bannisters is not because of outside power grabs and violence, but something else? What if I told you that they killed everyone else and took their power to fuel their spells—even your father, if you can call that man a father at all."

I'd say it was kind of an obvious statement, but Wren stumbled back a step. There was no love lost between them, still—to lose everyone for power...

Swallowing, she raised her chin. "Then, I'd say they have plenty of time to think about what they've done while they wait for their turn in Hell."

Oh, you sweet summer child.

"Are you fucking kidding me?" Nico rumbled, his eyes glowing with the gold of his wolf. "No. You don't leave a threat free to come back and kill you. They need to die, Wren. Now."

They argued for far too long, but in the end, Wren refused. Her gaze cut to Zephyr. "You can't use me as your weapon, and you can't manipulate me into meting out your revenge. I wasn't the one who made the deal. If you want to punish someone, punish them."

Zephyr's smile was once again a thing of nightmares. "You surprise me, child. I worried with Margot as your mother, you would be just as debased as she is. Then again, Áine did put an angel in your path, didn't she? You, my dear, have passed the test."

With that, he pressed the pad of his index finger against her forehead. Wren fell to her knees, and I called for my own power without a second thought. Nico held her to his chest as he yanked his wife from the demon prince. Theo shifted, the urge to protect them all too much. He and Ghost both launched themselves at Zephyr, his power knocking them away as if they were gnats.

"Stop it," I screamed, a spell full of darkness and hate forming in my palm. It would do shit against a demon, but no way was I going to stand by and let him hurt Wren. "You're killing her."

A snap of Zephyr's fingers later and the room went eerily silent. Wren's screams and Nico's yells, and Theo's growls—everything went away.

Including the giant demon prince and his stupid fucking magic. Nico gently shook Wren, his face a degree of devastation that I hadn't yet seen. We'd just gotten her back. No way could she be gone already.

Please, can we all just get one gods-damned break already?

"Bird?" Nico called, shaking her again. "Baby? Jesus Christ, Wren, are you okay?"

She peeled an eye open, then the other, and then she put her hand to his face, the Alpha visibly relaxing.

"I'm okay," she said, and she looked it. No blood, no exhaustion, just... Wren. "Let's get out of here, yeah?"

Nico pulled her to her feet and pressed a kiss to her temple while I felt like I was going to melt into a puddle on the floor. But then I caught sight of the very alive Bannister witches and readjusted my emotional map.

It seemed Nico, Theo, Ghost, and I were all on the same page because no one moved to follow her. None of us were going to let them live—not a one.

Nico gently pulled his hand from his wife's, shaking his head. "There are some things to button up here first. Go upstairs with Fiona. Theo and I will handle this."

The three witches were bemoaning their lost power, but Wren backed away from Nico like she'd never seen him before. "There is nothing to 'button up' down here. It's done."

But she didn't know what I knew. She didn't know that Nico had become a shell of a man with her gone. That he'd abandoned damn near every good thing about himself while he was forced to wait for her to return.

Nico was feral about his wife's safety—like pretty much all of us were now.

Nico's eye twitched as he set his jaw. "Do you think, as your husband, I will let a threat to your life live?"

"What threat?" Wren scoffed, pointing to her pitiful excuse of a family. "Three sobbing witches with no access to power?"

It was as if she pulled the pin on Nico's rage. And one by one, he neutralized Wren's family in the bloodiest way he possibly could right in front of us all. By the time he was done, the Bannister witches were no more.

I didn't mourn them. I'd learned long ago that

witches like that brought their fates upon themselves. And with them gone—if I took Zephyr at his word—I was free. The ABI wouldn't be looking for my power signature anymore. I wasn't going back to that cage again. I was...

So why didn't I feel it?

Why did not returning to the pack house seem like I was losing a home?

And why did the thought of not seeing Theo every day feel like I was losing myself?

12

THEO

Leaving the Bannister manor, I couldn't help the unease still lingering in my gut. Yes, the Bannister witches were dead. Wren's family was gone, and the pall they'd cast over the city of Savannah was likely gone with them as well.

But I had a feeling that Wren and Nico's relationship had taken a little hit. Maybe the pair would survive this, but an Alpha's relationship being tumultuous was never good for a pack.

Zephyr had touted an easy fix for Fiona's predicament by simply blaming the now-defunct Bannister Coven, but I doubted it would be that easy. That said, it wasn't like I could throw her in a cell that no longer existed. It wasn't like I could...

Glancing back at the cold manor, I wished someone would burn it down. There was too much pain here, too much unrest, and with the number of dead, it was too much to bury.

I had every intention of returning to the pack house, even though I had no idea what to do with myself. For the last four months, I had been tasked with keeping Fiona alive and safe, and I couldn't help but feel the need to keep with that tradition. And... a part of me felt like something was missing.

The purple-haired witch meandered away from the Bannister manor, heading toward Chatham Square, and instantly I knew what the missing thing was. Once upon a time, she'd had a beautiful little row house near that small patch of green. I could only assume she was heading there, and the thought of her leaving us made me want to break something.

"Where are you going? The pack house is this way." My tone was soft, but the burning need to keep her near me was eating me alive.

Her crystal-blue eyes flashed. "Why would I go back there?"

My hold on her bicep had been gentle. Her ripping it out of my grip was not. I figured Fiona didn't have any ill will toward us for locking her down, but maybe I was wrong.

"Sure, Wren is back, but that doesn't mean that the city isn't full of feral Fae and fucking demons. Just because you can practice magic now doesn't mean you're invincible."

Fiona hugged her arms to herself as if she was just as cold as she had been in that dungeon. "I know that, but I'm finally free. And... I kind of figured nobody would want me there."

As if my mother wouldn't claw my eyes out for leaving her behind. As if my sisters wouldn't beat me to a bloody pulp if I turned my back on her right now. Fiona was beloved not just by my family and my pack but by pretty much every single person that she came across. Malia and Hannah used to regularly tease that she could charm the most reluctant of people.

Or at least they did when she deigned to see them. They'd given her a pass when she'd been damn near dying. Now, not so much. Hell, even as much as I hated her kind and hated her family, she had still managed to charm me.

"Yeah, right. You having a teensy little pity party doesn't mean that you get to toss up a middle finger to everybody who has been worried sick about you since the day you opened that fucking gate—a gate of which that is still open, by the way."

Was that statement harsh as fuck? *Yes.*

That didn't stop it from being one hundred percent true.

"While I realize you're under the impression that the ABI won't be looking for you, it doesn't mean you can just waltz around like you're a god or something. Get your shit together, Jacobs."

Fiona shuffled back a step like I'd wounded her, but I just wanted her to listen to me for once. Just once I wanted her to really hear me.

"Oh, I'm Jacobs again, huh? What happened to Cupcake? Oh, that's right. You're only nice to me when I'm about to die, aren't you?"

Gritting my teeth, I grabbed her arm again, trying to guide her—not toward the pack house, but to mine, but she was too fast. She began walking backward, away from my home, away from the pack house, away... *from me.*

"You don't want to go and be around everybody who's been worried sick about you for years? That's fine. You can come to my house while you lick your wounds and pretend that you aren't embarrassed for the mistakes you've made."

Fiona spun on her heel, stomping away this time like her ass was on fire.

"Oh, fuck you, Theo." Angrily, she tossed up her hands, her fingertips sparking as her emotions got away from her. "How was I supposed to know what she was and what deal her she-beast of a mother made?"

Fiona spun again. This time, she poked my chest with her sparking finger, singeing the fabric of my designer shirt.

"I didn't see you helping out. I didn't see you opening a damn gate. I didn't see you trying to get her back. Yeah, it's real obvious you don't really give a shit about your brother's happiness, you asshole."

Her words speared me in a way that brought all the shame I had been holding down rearing its ugly head.

"Fuck me, huh? We're only in this mess because of you."

That wasn't exactly true.

We were in this mess because a Fae Prince wanted to stick it to his daddy, but that was beside the point.

She was the one who opened the Hell gate.

She was the one who set Zephyr free.

She was the catalyst that knocked over the first domino in the shit pie that was Savannah.

And she thought she was going to walk away? She thought she wasn't going to face what she'd done? She thought she was going to leave?

Once again, Fiona ripped her touch away from me, setting my teeth on edge.

"You really need to make up your mind. One second, I'm Cupcake and Fiona, we're playing *Clue*, and you give a shit that my favorite color is green. Now you're blaming me for things you know I paid for." Tears welled in her eyes, making me feel about two inches tall. "I was in that cell for four months, Theo. Four. Unable to do magic, unable to eat as those bars ate away at everything I was. You're pissed you got stuck with me? Fine. You're pissed that I'm free? I can't help that, but you don't get to keep blaming me. And I don't have to walk into that pack house and watch everybody do the same."

"That's real rich coming from you."

Fiona had refused to see Malia and Hannah, hell, she'd actually refused to see *anyone*, but my sisters were relentless and refused to be denied. I don't know what kind of reception she would get in the pack, but with their Alpha's mate returned, I had a feeling things would be forgiven.

Wouldn't they?

"I'm not pissed that you're free. I'm fucking worried sick," I barked, the words just coming out of me of their own accord. "Just because Wren healed you doesn't mean you're okay."

Because what if she hadn't really detoxed from the

black magic? What if it was still poisoning her? What if one of those Fae took her like they'd taken Wren? What if someone hurt her? What if...

What if she died?

That was the real rub, wasn't it? History repeating itself.

"Excuse me for giving a shit that I don't want to see you walk away from the closest thing to a family you have here," I whispered, regretting every word that forced its way out of my mouth. "The city is still locked down. We're all you got."

It wasn't exactly true. If she could explain away a four-month absence to the ABI, and on the off chance they weren't looking for the gate-opener anymore, she could have them as well.

Not that I'd tell her that.

"Well, lucky me, I've got a wolfy babysitter who thinks he's my fucking keeper." She sneered, clasping her hands together as if in prayer. "Just what I always wanted." Rolling her eyes, she shook her head. "No, thanks, Theo. I'm pretty sure I've got it from here."

She didn't have it. She didn't have that first fucking clue. Snarling, I latched on to her delicate wrist as she turned and reeled her in.

I couldn't say what made me do it. Maybe it was the fear. Maybe it was the need to keep her close—to keep her safe. Or maybe it was that I had been denying myself for so long that I'd just gone crazy.

One second, I was so mad I was seeing red, and the next, I was yanking her to me and pressing my lips to hers.

Fiona froze—her whole body rigid for one long moment until the silk of her tongue flitted across my bottom lip. Somehow, I remained standing even though my heart tried to beat its way out of my chest.

I pressed her body against mine, managing to keep my eyes from rolling back into my skull. Her soft curves barely brushed against my chest, but I couldn't get enough. Her breath mingled with mine, and I wanted to bathe in it.

If I kissed her again, I knew I wouldn't be able to stop. If I wrapped my arms around her, I wouldn't let her go, and if I ever sank into her hot, wet heat, I'd never come up for air.

She pulled away just a little, her brilliant blue gaze boring into me in a way that made me want to give her anything.

Everything.

I was so fucked.

My grip found its way to her chin, my thumb rubbing that plump bottom lip I wanted to bite so bad I was willing to kill someone to do it. It was a delicate rosy pink, and I was dying to know if her nipples would be the same color.

Would her pussy? My cock jumped against my zipper at the thought.

"You're coming home with me." It wasn't a question, and I didn't phrase it like one. It was a demand, an order, and Fiona took it like a challenge.

"And what if I say no?" she asked on a whisper, her mouth millimeters from mine. The question was both seductive and galling all at the same time.

I couldn't help it, I nipped at that bottom lip, sucking it into my mouth, tasting it.

"Do you *want* to say no?" My hands cupped her ass, nearly lifting her off her feet as I pulled her tight against me, trapping my hardness between us. Fiona's eyes flared with heat as she let out the tiniest of whimpers. "I don't think you do. I think you want me to fuck you until you can't walk straight the next day. I think you want me to lick you until you come all over my face."

I dipped my head, raking my nose up her neck, aching to taste her there. She smelled so fucking good...

"But you have to say yes, Cupcake. You want this as much as I do. Admit it."

Please don't say no. Please don't say no. Please don't say no.

I couldn't remember the last time I had a woman in

my arms. Couldn't remember the last time I'd even wanted someone like this. *Not since...*

Don't think about her.

I deserved an ounce of peace, or at the very least, to scratch this itch. Maybe if I got Fiona out of my system, I could think again.

I could breathe.

Fiona's fingers fisted in my shirt, yanking me closer, even though the only way we *could* be closer was if we were naked.

"I want this," she breathed, the words so faint it was a wonder I heard them at all.

"Say it again," I ordered, lifting her off her feet. Immediately, she wrapped her legs around me, and the heat of her center nearly took me to my knees. "Now, Cupcake. Tell me."

Her blue eyes flashed with a smolder so hot it burned me to the quick. I wanted that same look on her face when I sank into her.

"I want you."

And that was all I needed to hear.

13

FIONA

I didn't know what possessed me to follow Theo to his house on the other side of Forsyth Park. Maybe it was the heat of him against me when I'd been so cold for so long. Maybe it was the way his giant hand engulfed mine as he pulled me behind him, his hold so gentle and so strong. I knew he could play me like an instrument if he put his mind to it.

Or maybe it was because I craved him like a fucking junkie and always had.

Before I knew it, we walked up a set of porch stairs to a pretty midnight-blue door I barely saw. The inside of his home was black as pitch, and I knew he could see everything in the dark even though I couldn't. It was almost like being blindfolded, the illicit little bit of danger making the need in my middle double in size.

As soon as the door closed behind us, Theo picked me up like I weighed nothing—to him, I probably didn't— and set my ass on a hard surface, fitting his body between my open legs. My breath hitched at the full-body contact, the electricity pulsing between us like a live wire.

But better? His breath hitched, too. He wanted me just as much as I wanted him. I was willing to bet on it.

A moment later, his lips brushed mine—soft at first before turning hungry, demanding, owning my mouth like it was a mere preview of how he'd own the rest of me. My breasts ached as they pressed against his hard chest, so heavy it was as if they were begging for his hands on them, too.

His fingers found their way under my sweater, his blazing touch against my skin smooth as silk and gentle as a whisper.

But I didn't want gentle.

I didn't want nice.

And as if he was reading my mind, he fisted his hands in the fabric and ripped, tearing it up the middle to expose my bra. Theo let loose a long low growl, the vibration of it making me shiver with want. My legs tightened around him, pulling him in, pulling him closer, almost begging in a way I wouldn't let myself otherwise.

"*Fuck*," he murmured. "You're so fucking pretty."

He trailed a finger over the swell of one of my breasts before hooking it into the fabric. The gentle scrape of what could only be a talon raked across a nipple before catching the center of my bra and ripping it in two.

Exposed.

In the dark.

I felt his eyes on me even though I couldn't see him. It was as if he was kissing every inch of me, worshipping every square inch of bare skin.

I fisted my hands in his suit jacket, yanking it down his arms. Theo got with the program, peeling out of that damn jacket while I worked on the buttons of his shirt. A snap of my fingers later, and they went flying, pinging against the floor in every direction.

"I want to see you," I whispered, the dark room making me miss all the good bits. "Let me see you."

A second later, he pulled away, leaning over until I heard a gentle click of the lamp. Then he was back, towering over me, his ever-present tie long gone. His white designer shirt hung wide open, exposing the skin underneath. Like a greedy kid in a candy shop, I yanked the fabric from his shoulders, relishing every inch of golden, inked skin, loving the way it stretched so tight over his muscles.

Theo was always in a suit, and damn if they just

didn't do him justice. He needed to be naked all the time, or at least never wear a shirt again. I wanted to trace all the ink with my tongue.

When I finally peeled my eyes from his chest, I met his gaze, and the heat in them burned me from the inside out.

"You keep looking at me like that, Cupcake, and we won't make it out of this room."

Fine by me. "Who says I want to leave this room?"

Because I didn't want to leave this room. If I had my way, he'd fuck me on this desk, right there and right then.

The green of his wolf lit in his eyes, showing me just how turned on he was, and I practically squirmed in anticipation.

His fingers fisted in the fabric of my lounge pants. "Last chance, Cupcake," he warned roughly. "If you want out, you'd better tell me now."

But I couldn't think of a good reason not to be there.

Okay, that was a lie.

I could think of approximately eight thousand reasons why fucking Theo Acosta would be the worst idea I had ever had. Too bad the sensible part of my brain was firmly toggled in the "Off" position. I was a mess of needy wants and baser instincts, and those instincts wanted Theo to rip off my clothes and fuck me until I couldn't breathe.

Naturally, I taunted the big lug.

"What? You too scared to show me what you've got, wolf? I believe I was promised to walk funny tomorrow. You chickening out?"

A second later, my pants and underwear were in shreds, and I was flat on my back on the desk, Theo's growl and the cold wood against my naked skin making me tremble. His strong hands spread me wide before yanking me to the edge of the desk.

"No surrender then," he murmured, kneeling between my legs. "Remember that when you're begging me to let you come."

He kissed the delicate flesh of my inner thigh, nipping it, licking it, and I fought off the urge to moan. "And you will beg," he whispered, his lips rubbing against my skin with every word. "I promise you that."

Then his breath feathered over my sex, making my whole body quake, and damn if I didn't lose already. A whimper broke free of my iron control, and I couldn't find a fuck to give. Not. One.

I would say this: Theo didn't tease.

As soon as he put his mind to fucking me, he got down to the business of it. He played me like a fiddle, his tongue curling around my clit before sucking it into his mouth. My back bowed at the targeted pleasure, a moan squeezing out of my throat before I could even stop it.

His thick, blunt fingers played with the slick wetness of my sex before filling me, stretching me, wringing another moan out of me with minimal effort. Then he curled those gorgeous fingers, touching a place inside me that made me want to promise him anything if he just didn't stop. My fingers scrabbled for purchase, aching to hold on to something, *anything*, before Theo caught them, guiding them to his hair, his gaze so piercing that I nearly stopped breathing.

"These hands belong here. If you need something to hold onto, you hold onto me. Got it?"

As if answering his command, I fisted my fingers in the strands, grounding myself in him as he went back to trying to murder me. Okay, if this was how I was going to go, it was a good one and a far sight better than any other end I'd envisioned for myself.

Because he *was* killing me. Slowly, carefully, hungrily. I was dying. I couldn't breathe, I couldn't... But I could breathe because I was moaning, pleading with him to do... something...

"Make me come," I ordered, my breathless pants doing nothing to enforce that command.

And damn if I didn't feel his smile against my skin as he continued his torture, his growl of approval vibrating against me in the most delicious way. When I tried lifting my hips, he held me down with one powerful arm, the dark tattoos against my skin so fucking sexy I thought I was going to pass out.

"I didn't hear that. Say it again," he rumbled, and I would have said anything to get his mouth back where it belonged.

"Make me come. *Please*," I ground out through gritted teeth.

His smile was sinister. "You can do better than that. Ask me nicely. No. *Beg* me to make you come."

Theo twisted his fingers, continuing his torture, even though his mouth was mere inches away from where I wanted it.

"Please, Theo," I whispered. "*Please*. I need it."

When he returned his mouth to my sex, I saw stars. Honestly, the orgasm snuck up on me. One second, I was begging like my life depended on it, and the next, I was damn near screaming as beautiful heat washed over me from head to toe, knocking me for a loop as I melted into a puddle on the desk.

I couldn't recall a single orgasm—accompanied or otherwise—that wrecked me so well.

It was a struggle to peel my eyes open, but *the view*... Theo rose to his feet, his strong hands removing his belt with the sexiest slap of leather imaginable before unbuttoning his trousers. He shoved them down, taking his boxer briefs with them to expose the thickest, most beautiful cock I had ever seen in my life.

No wonder Theo was a cocky motherfucker. No wonder he said I'd be walking funny. He had a damn cannon in his pants. I would be lucky to have the use of my legs at all.

Instantly, I ached. Everything in me cried out in want for this man. I needed his hands everywhere, his mouth, his cock. And I wanted to taste him, hear him, beg for him.

Somehow, I gained the wherewithal to sit up, my hands reaching for him as though I were pulled by a string. My fingertips traced the swirls of ink that spread across his chest, and I reveled in the stilted breaths he took at my touch. But something about it seemed too precious, too serious, too...

"I remember some mighty big promises coming out of that mouth," I taunted. "Care to back them up?"

Theo's gaze was damn near predatory as he yanked my hips to the edge of the desk before flipping me over, his arm banding across my chest to keep me from smacking my face into the wood. His fingers plucked at a single aching nipple, tearing a gasp out of me.

"Anyone ever tell you that you have a smart mouth?" he growled in my ear as he fit his cock to my opening.

I wanted to answer him—I did—but before I could,

he pressed inside, stealing all thought, all breath. There was nothing to do except feel him own me, thrust after thrust.

"Fuck, look at you taking me," he groaned, the vibration of it doing me in.

The pleasure built, filling me until I was hanging onto his arm for purchase. The sweat of his chest against my back, his groans, his harsh breaths, all of it. I couldn't have held onto my release if I tried.

Just like before, it caught me off guard, pulling me under until I was drowning. The long, low growl of his release sent aftershocks rolling through me, and only then did I wilt to the cool desktop. Sucking in panting breaths, I tried to focus, tried to make my legs hold me up, but the day had been too much.

Theo had been too much.

So when he carried me to his bed, I didn't so much as complain.

For once.

And when he tucked me in beside him and turned out his light, I had the best sleep I'd had in years.

Too bad I knew I was going to fuck it up.

14

FIONA

I shouldn't have been surprised to wake up alone, but I was.

It was stupid. Whatever happened the night before with Theo was just some bullshit we needed to get out of our system—a fleeting thing that probably shouldn't ever be repeated. I mean, this was Theo we were talking about. As long as he'd known me, he'd hated my guts.

Why would that change?

I shouldn't have been even a little surprised—shouldn't have felt cold all over again, like I was still back in that stupid fucking cell.

But I *was* cold and naked, and I felt so, so stupid.

What was I thinking? I'd just had sex with Nico's older brother—with Wren's brother-in-law. I didn't even know how old he was. I didn't... There was so much I didn't know about Theo—so much he would never tell me.

This was dumb. *I* was dumb. And I didn't even have any clothes to wear for a walk of shame. My whole body did a little shudder as I remembered just what happened to my clothes the night before. How he'd torn them from my body. How he'd kissed every inch of me. How he'd made me beg...

There was a teensy, tiny, little, minuscule part of me that still wanted him—that had always wanted him. The part that thought he was strong and loyal and devious and not some boy-in-blue, Goody two-shoes sycophant with a stick up his ass. Well, Theo *always* had a stick up his ass, but I sort of liked that about him.

He had just the right amount of grey. He'd kill for the ones he loved. He'd fight. I could respect a man like that.

Too bad he would never respect me.

The clang of a pot brought my attention to the open door, and I quickly examined what had to be Theo's bedroom. The moldings and tray ceiling had to be from at least the 1800s. In the middle of the room sat a giant canopy bed with gossamer curtains gathered at the posts. There was a writing desk in the corner and a chaise near the cold fireplace.

Every part of Theo's room looked like it was from a different century. It was that stuffy, cultured bit that preferred suits to jeans and designer to commercial. I had half a mind to go through his closet and see if it would be wall-to-wall suits. Maybe I'd find his stash of pocket squares and ties.

Maybe I'd throw them all in the garbage.

Another clang rang out, and I wondered if the kitchen was rising up against its owner. With nothing for it, I yanked the top sheet off the bed, fashioned myself a toga, and tiptoed out of the room. At the first landing, I took a right, heading downstairs toward the busy kitchen.

Peeking around the corner, I saw a broad, tattooed back at what had to be the biggest stove I'd ever seen. The swirls of ink on Theo's back barely covered a mishmash of deep scars. They scored into the flesh, pitted in some places and rough in others. It didn't matter how beautiful or cleverly placed the artwork was, whatever had been done to Theo had been horrendous.

I couldn't think of a single thing that could do that to a wolf and not kill him. Shifters healed at a rapid rate, the liminal spaces that called their animal, feeding into the magic of their bodies. Wolves didn't scar, so whatever had been done to him was so far past barbaric, it made me ill.

A searing sort of rage filled my gut, overtaking the stupidity and self-deprecating flair I'd had earlier. At that very moment, it did not matter that Theo probably didn't want me. It didn't matter that I was a Jacobs witch. Hell, it didn't even matter who his brother was or what I was doing in this kitchen.

I wanted to know what had happened to Theo, and I wanted to know right then.

Swallowing hard, I held my tongue. I might have even had to bite it, drawing just a little blood so I wouldn't fly off the handle.

"Have a seat, Cupcake," Theo ordered, not even turning around as he nearly startled me out of my skin. "I hope you like pancakes. You're not allergic to almonds, right?"

Woodenly, I took a seat at the bar, only slightly miffed that he knew I was there the whole time. "No, I'm not allergic to anything. But why the almonds?"

He shrugged, dumping another pancake on a plate. "I'm not here that often, and the only shelf-stable milk I had was almond milk. I went to the market while you were sleeping and managed to get eggs, but nobody had any milk. I guess the ABI is falling down on the job letting shipments in."

He turned off the burner and pivoted with two plates

in his hands, setting them on the bar between us. "You would think they would be better at locking down a city."

I couldn't say whether the ABI was good at locking down any city. I hadn't exactly been party to this one. A part of me wondered if they'd assumed I'd gone AWOL or if I'd died. But getting up to date with my employer was not high on my list of tasks. Finding out what the fuck had happened to Theo was.

Well, that, and closing a Hell gate—not that I knew how to do either of those things.

It took me a second—maybe because I was too focused on whatever had happened to his back—but my brain finally registered that Theo had made me breakfast. He hadn't told me to leave or that he was disgusted that we'd had sex or anything of the sort.

Theo Acosta was making me morning-after-sex breakfast.

That had to be one for the record books, right? I mean, this giant, tattooed fucking god in the sack was making me breakfast while I lounged in a sheet toga on his barstool. I was probably hallucinating. None of the events of the last twenty-four hours had ever happened, and I would wake up any time now.

Any time now.

Twenty seconds later, I had a plateful of silver-dollar

pancakes in front of me that looked so good I was afraid to eat them.

Theo stared at me like I was a few crayons shy of a full box. "You do like pancakes, right?"

That had me sitting back on my stool and blinking at him like he was the crazy one. "Who doesn't like pancakes?"

"Crazy people. Crazy people don't like pancakes. You're not a crazy person, are you?" Theo asked, utterly deadpan, his expression so stoic, it was hilarious.

Smiling, I picked up my fork, stabbed a pancake, and shoved it in my mouth. I swallowed, waggling my hand. "That's debatable, but I do love pancakes."

His gorgeous eyes flashed green, a slow smile tipping up the edges of his lips into an almost smile. Theo didn't smile very often. In fact, the only time I could ever remember his mouth with a full grin was right before he'd made me beg him to fuck me silly.

I supposed I would just have to take this ghost of a smile.

What had happened to this man to harden him this way—to make him so closed off? Was it those scars on his back? Was it his father? His family? Did they hurt him?

The pancake in my mouth turned to sawdust, and I put down my fork.

"What happened?" I asked, and there was no way for him to gauge the context of my question. I didn't elaborate. I wanted information, and I was blindly seeking it.

He frowned, his smile slipping. "What do you mean? What happened with what? What happened last night? Between us? You're going to have to be more specific."

Swallowing, I managed not to scream. "What happened to your back, Theo? The tattoos are beautiful, but they don't hide as much as you think they do. What happened to your back?"

Theo's entire face shuddered in an instant, his jaw clenching as his eyes turned cold. He backed away from the bar and yanked a dark blue button-up from a hook I hadn't noticed nearby. He shrugged into the shirt and began buttoning it.

What he did not do in any way, shape, or form was answer me.

"I've spent every single day with you for four months," I reminded him. "Why don't I know more about you? Why don't I know about this?"

"There's nothing to tell. Nothing happened to me." He stared at the stone counter, refusing to meet my eyes. "Eat your food."

I dropped my fork, letting it clang against the plate. "Don't fucking lie to me. Something happened, and I want to know who I need to kill. Cough it up, Acosta. I want a name."

His shoulders seemed to swell in size as his eyes blazed with his wolf.

"And I just spent the last four months watching you starve and nearly fucking die, so eat your gods-damned food."

He yanked his still-full plate off the bar and dumped it in the sink, turning his now-covered back to me. "Maybe you don't know that much about me because there isn't much to know. I was my father's second, and now I'm Nico's. I do what needs doing. I hold this family together, and that's all there is. That's all there ever is."

I wanted to slap whoever had told him that.

"Bullshit. There's more to you than that. Where's the guy who reads old cowboy novels and plays *Clue*? Where's that guy? Because that's the guy who fucked me last night, not the second-in-command Theo. Not your brother's right hand. Not a single thing you just said. *That guy* is my friend. That guy kept me alive. I don't know the man you claim to be, but I do know the man you are."

Theo flipped the plate in the sink, breaking it. "You don't know shit. You want to know what happened? Your father. That's what happened to my fucking back."

That had me rocking on the stool, scrabbling for purchase on the bar so I didn't dump myself over.

"What?" I breathed, my vision tunneling just a bit.

My father had done a lot of things, but torturing a wolf hadn't ever been one of them. But that didn't mean...

"Do you want to know why there's nothing else? Your father took it from me. I'm over a century old, and I don't have a mate," he admitted, his voice deepening to a growl so sinister it froze me to the spot. "Do you want to know why? Because your father fucking killed her."

Shaking my head, I tried to deny it, but...

"Wolves get the mating call at thirty, but mine didn't come because she wasn't born yet. So I didn't get it until she came of age. When I went looking for her, you want to know what I found? A burned-out wreck of a house. Didn't stop me from going in, though."

It was as if the whole world was swallowing me up. Theo could have been happy, could have been free... In my head, I saw him smiling, saw him with kids and a faceless wife that he adored. And even though it wasn't true, it still made my chest ache.

"That's when I found out that the house had been destroyed by a curse," he continued, his tale flowing out of him now. "A curse that damn near killed me as I tried to pull my mate from the wreckage. It took years, but I found out who did it, who killed her, but there wasn't anything I could do. Nothing that wouldn't start a war, and it wasn't like I could prove it or bring her back. So I got stuck being my father's second, being my brother's right-hand man, being *this*. No life, no wife, nothing but doing what I'm ordered to do day in and day out for the rest of this cursed fucking existence."

He swallowed, his hands nearly trembling as they fisted at his sides.

"So when you ask me what happened to my back, I want you to understand that it's none of your fucking business."

There was so much disgust on his face, so much... Had this all...

"Did you—was I revenge?" That hollow feeling that had made itself a home in my chest when I'd woken up by myself yawned wide. "Did you put me in that cell for revenge? Did you—"

"What? Screw you as a way to screw your daddy? No, Fiona, even I'm not that evil."

My nose burned, and my eyes welled with tears, but I wouldn't let them fall. I *wouldn't*.

"I don't believe you," I whispered, choking on the despair in my chest. "I asked what happened to you because I actually give a shit. Because I wanted to know who had hurt you, but it does make a sick sort of sense.

You've hated me from day one. It doesn't matter how many rounds of *Clue* we played or that I know your favorite color. I still don't know that first thing about you. But I am glad you got that one last 'fuck you' to my father. By the state of your back, it looks like you've earned it."

Theo's sneer should have been classified as a deadly weapon. It sure as hell was killing me then. "Believe what you want, but eat your fucking breakfast. I didn't watch you almost starve to death for months only to watch you keep doing it now."

Then he turned his back on me, yanking a fresh suit jacket off a chair and striding out of the room. The front door slammed a moment later, shaking the whole house in his wake.

Luckily for me, he didn't see the first tear fall, or the tenth, or the hundredth. By the time I was done crying my eyes out, I was so mad I could barely see straight. As much as I wanted to bash Theo's stupid skull in, I wanted vengeance on my father more.

But first, I needed clothes.

Ultimately, I wound up using Theo's landline to call Hannah. I for damn sure could not call Wren, and if I called one of Theo's sisters, they would know instantly what I'd done and who I'd done it with. I didn't *want* to call Malia or Hannah. I had pretty much ignored them for the last four months, choosing to have my pity party in my cell alone rather than be with my friends.

"Oh, so you only call when you need something. That's rich," Hannah jeered down the line.

"Look," I hissed, wiping the last of my tears off my face. "I am currently naked in a guy's house with no access to clothes, and unless I want to do a sheet-toga-style walk of shame, I am pretty much fucked. Now, I would love to explain why my throwing a four-month-long pity party was probably the height of a depressive episode, but I'm going to need you to arrive with a boatload of clothes first."

There was silence for a good long minute.

"I'm bringing Malia with me, and there's not a damn thing you can do about it."

Rolling my eyes, I fought off the urge to stomp my foot. "I sort of figured. Just don't tell Wren, will you? She's got enough on her plate. Plus, in all likelihood, she's diddling Nico or figuring out the secrets of the universe or something. The last thing she needs is to find out that I'm screwing her brother-in-law."

"Which brother-in-law? The one you spent four months in a dungeon with, maybe?"

"What do you think?"

Hannah snorted out a derisive laugh. "I'll be there in

ten minutes with Malia, and the cranky psychic told me to tell you there had better be pancakes left."

True to her word, Malia and Hannah arrived twelve minutes later with an entire suitcase in hand. I could have hugged them both, but I had a feeling the giant ghoul might attempt to eat me, and not in a good way.

Malia snaked around Hannah, her dainty arms encased in gloves. Malia was a psychometry witch—an oracle of sorts—who could see the past, present, and future of everything she touched. It made her a teensy bit crazy, but we wouldn't have her any other way.

"Four months of no contact, and we get a toga party? I'm going to need some details and a big fucking apology, you shithead. We were worried sick about you."

I snatched the suitcase right out of Hannah's hands, clutching it to my chest like it was the key to my every wish. The laugh that came out of me was utterly mirthless and a little crazy.

"Details? Well, let's see. I murdered twelve witches to gain enough power to open a gate, which failed. Instead, I opened a Hell gate and brought a Prince of Hell to this plane along with a shit-ton of demons. I was imprisoned for four months under a null ward that damn near killed me, unable to eat or drink or do anything but be stuck with a wolf who has a vendetta against my family. A wolf I may have accidentally fucked last night within an inch of my life. Then we had the mother of all blowout fights this morning after he made me pancakes."

Malia blinked, and Hannah shuffled back a step as her blue eyes went wide.

"Now is that enough detail, or can I get dressed?"

I knew things wouldn't be forgiven so easily. I knew I owed them more than just a single bullshit explanation and a shrug of my shoulders.

But my heart had just gotten broken.

And I was pretty sure I was still half in love with the person who had broken it.

THEO

I should have known when I finally took something for myself, it would all go to shit. I had one night of happiness. One single, solitary evening where I didn't worry for my brother or my family. Where I didn't think about anyone or anything but the woman in my arms.

That was my curse, wasn't it? For everything I touched to fall apart?

Why else would Fiona think I only bedded her to get back at her father?

Why else would she pick at the one loose thread that reminded me why I hated her family?

And why was I staring at my brother's wife doing crazy witchy spell shit on our back lawn?

I'd left Fiona alone in my house without a stitch of clothing to her name, only to return to the shitshow that was the Acosta pack. Wyatt, my brother's best friend—and the man who most definitely should be second instead of me—had gotten it into his fool head that the best way to close the Hell gate was to open the Fae one.

Or maybe that idea was Wren's.

And if Nico was the Alpha of our pack—our King—then Wren was his Queen and had just as much power as he did. So that meant telling her no was pretty much out of the question.

Closing the gate meant something different to me than it did to everyone else. Closing it meant Fiona would be safe, keeping her pretty little neck away from an executioner's sword. Wren probably cared about the city being under possession by a sea of demons. All I cared about was Fiona.

Of course she thinks you fucked her to get back at her family. Those bastards are all she knows. Moves and countermoves.

If this pack were anything like Fiona's family, I'd probably have believed it, too.

But that pissed me off. Didn't she trust me by now? Didn't she... *know*, deep down in her bones, that I had done nothing but protect her day in and day out for months? Which was why I was watching Wren instead of standing in her way.

My witchy sister-in-law stood in the middle of a sigil burned into the back lawn, having summoned the one motherfucker we could not find. Suspended midair was Tristan—or rather, Drystan Haldrir Shadowfall, Crown Prince of the Dark Court. A coating of blackness held his arms and legs immobile while another snake of black fire collared his neck.

Naturally, all this happened while Nico was taking a well-deserved rest—something he hadn't done in the three years Wren had been gone. No one in their right mind would have woken him... though maybe one of us should have.

Stomping out of the back door, he made a beeline for his wife with the most probable intention of snatching her ass out of the very real, very powerful circle she was in.

Both Wyatt and I stopped him, pointing up at the completely immobile royal asshole. Tristan gulped for air like a fish out of water, and then all at once, he fell to the ground, his bonds pulling at his limbs as if he were being stretched by four invisible horses.

After four months of being free but stuck topside and nowhere to run in this city, the Fae seemed a hell of a lot better off than he should have been. There was no getting out of Savannah—not without a damn good ABI deal under his belt, and I seriously doubted he'd get one of those. The ABI was notorious for not dealing with the Fae as a rule. Still, he was dressed in clean clothes, and though his cheeks were sharp and his scars bright, he seemed better off than he should.

My gaze tracked to Mariella in the sea of pack surrounding the Fae. If there was one person in Savannah that would help him survive, it would definitely be her—a secret I'd kept for no other reason than I couldn't watch her lose everything like I had. My mate had been a witch. What if her mate was this fuck-wad of a Fae?

What if I stole that from her?

I'd never forgive myself.

But that didn't make me too eager to stop what was happening right then.

"Now, Drystan—you don't mind if I call you by the name your mama gave you, now, do you?" Wren asked, her voice as deadly as a snake and sweet as sugar. "Well, Áine and I go way back—all the way to my childhood when she helped me come home. Gave me blessings and everything. She's also the one who helped me out of the Dark Court this time."

Wren clucked her tongue, her voice carrying a thicker

accent as she let him know just how much he'd fucked up.

"You see, me being there is not a good idea. If it isn't your daddy hating me, well, my mere presence seems to cause a problem with the fabric of reality as we know it. As in, me being in the Fae realm doesn't just destroy the Dark Court—like I suspect you knew it would—it breaks the Seelie Court as well."

Oh. Oh, shit. Had Wren not returned when she did, the Fae realm would have ceased to exist at all. It would have killed all of them and their magic. It would have killed *her*.

That got Tristan's attention. "My mother. Is she all right?"

"You selfish fuck," Nico growled, nearly losing the hold on his animal. "Is that all you care about?"

The Fae stared at him incredulously. "Is not your wife all you cared about? She is my family. Why is that any different?"

"Because my wife was helpless against you." Nico's eyes glowed gold, his wolf roiling under his skin, and if that Fae knew what was good for him, he'd stop antagonizing my brother before he ripped him apart.

Tristan raised an eyebrow. "Well, she's not helpless now."

"No, Sweet Pea, I'm not. But I do need your help, so

I'll offer you an exchange." Wren snapped her fingers, the bonds around Tristan's neck, wrists, and ankles melting away. "You help me open the Fae gates worldwide, and I promise to never summon you again. No torture, no pain, no grudges."

"Speak for yourself," Wyatt, Nico, and I said at the same time.

Wren raised an eyebrow. "Yeah, but he isn't scared of you, now, is he? He's scared of me. Because he knows I could rip him limb from limb and make it stick. Or I could call on a Prince of Hell to haul his dumb ass on down to have a chat. Mr. Tristan thinks I am a destroyer of worlds, and while I could be, I have no interest in that particular pastime."

She focused on Tristan, her expression just a touch wrong as she leveled him with her sweetest smile. "Now, do we have a deal, Sugar Plum, or am I going to have to get creative with my incentive? I guarantee I am meaner than my husband. I'll make what your daddy did to you look like fucking Disneyland."

Her eyes lit with twin flames, her green-gold irises changing to orange so fast it scared the shit out of me. She was bluffing. Or at least I *hoped* she was bluffing. *Please don't let this woman be any more dangerous than she already is.*

"Tik tock, Tinkerbell. I have problems to solve."

Tristan scanned the yard filled with my brothers and sisters and the majority of the pack. His gaze stuttered on Mariella, and the pair shared a long look before she nodded.

Fuck. My sister's eyes were filled with tears, and she made herself turn her back on him.

"Fine." He stepped closer to Wren, his voice going low, but I still heard: "I will help you open the gates, but you know what will happen. You know what he'll do."

Somehow between him taking his first step and his last word, Nico had Tristan's throat in his taloned hand and his feet off the ground. Nico had crossed Wren's circle and latched onto him so fast that no one could have stopped him. And as much as I would have loved to watch my brother squeeze the life out of him, it would kill Mari.

But Nico didn't kill him. No, he warned him instead. "You so much as look at her wrong, and I will make sure whatever punishment she dreams up becomes a reality. I know you don't care about pain, so I'll use my imagination."

Tristan's smug smile was far less confident than I expected it to be. "You could try, wolf, but your bride is correct. I fear her a lot more than I fear you."

"Let him down, Nico. He needs his voice if he wants

to open the gates, and it's not like I can substitute him for another Fae. Trust me—I checked."

Nico released the dipshit and backed up a step. "Sure thing, Bird."

Tristan stared at his feet. "I can't open the Fae doors."

Wren laughed—her giggle sweet as if she thought he was adorable. "Of course you can't. You borrowed your father's magic to do it, didn't you? I bet with all his playthings, he didn't even notice when you siphoned it off of him. It didn't matter how much they tortured you. You were never opening those gates. Right?"

Two and a half years. Two and a half fucking years, and he... I had half a mind to kill him myself.

Tristan took a healthy step away from Wren. "How in the blue bloody fuck do you know that?"

Wren pointed to the delicate skin beside her eye. "I can see better this time around. I bet you wished I was still the naïve little child falling for illusion mage's tricks, now, don't you?"

His lips twisted. "It would certainly help." His sigh sounded like he was trying to let his soul escape before Wren got ahold of it. "Fine. Do you have a plan, or are our asses just swinging in the wind?"

"Of course I do. But we need a change of venue."

With a single snap of her fingers, we were on the edges of Chatham Square, its burning gate still going even four months later. Wren, Nico, Ghost, and Tristan stood in the middle of the blaze, the fire not touching them.

Wren sucked in a deep breath, and then it was as if all the fire in the entire square filled her lungs. The never-ending flames flickered and died, their heat melting away on the breeze. The Hell gate stood tall for all the world to see, but it wasn't on fire anymore.

But Wren seemed to be made of it. Flames danced in her eyes as her red hair failed to follow the rules of gravity, floating in the air in a nimbus cloud around her head. And that didn't even touch the fact that she was hovering at eye level with Tristan.

Movement peeled my gaze away, and at the edge of the square were Fiona, Hannah, and Malia. Fiona's blue eyes were wide as she watched her best friend levitate six inches off the ground, the fire living on her skin instead of the trees. Then her eyes flicked to Tristan, and it was as if the rage she'd been holding onto snapped. Hannah wrapped her arms around her, plucking Fiona off the ground like she was a child.

Four months ago, Fiona had barely been able to contain the blaze to this little patch of earth. But I had a feeling if Hannah wasn't holding her back, she would rip Tristan's spine right out of his body.

I weaved through the crowd, trying to get to Fiona

before she did something she'd regret, shoving people out of my way when they wouldn't move—the lot of them too captivated by whatever Wren was doing.

Somehow, I made it to her, ripping Fiona from Hannah's hold and into mine. She tried to claw her way out of my arms, but I held her tighter.

"Stop it," I hissed, tightening my hold. "She needs him to open the Fae gates—only then can you close the Hell one."

Fiona stilled, her chest heaving as she watched Wren, Nico, and Tristan open the gate.

A vine-covered door shimmered into being amongst the still-smoking grass and ruined trees. Flowers bloomed on the vines, a bright spot of color in the midst of the blackness. But more than that, it was as if the world itself took a breath, as if someone had opened a window in a stuffy house, and now the air flowed freely.

"You're not done," Wren snarled, yanking him closer, her words barely audible over the murmurs of the pack. "As payment for fixing your fuck-up and lending you my power, you will bring me the forty-three women that your father stole."

What? She's letting him go? I didn't dare relay that to Fiona, only met Nico's gaze across the square.

"What? No." Tristan yanked at his arm in her grip, but Wren didn't so much as budge. The smell of burning flesh hit my nose an instant before Tristan fell to his knees, Wren's feet touching the ground for the first time in minutes.

"*Yes.* I can't go into the Fae realm without destroying it," she hissed, pulling Tristan to her in an iron grip. "As much as I would love to watch your father get crushed beneath his absolute *cliché* of a castle, I need those women back more. You get them out, and we'll be square."

Tristan howled as a flame flickered over Wren's hand, only getting louder as her fire-like gaze grew brighter. "Fulfill this bargain, and no member of the Acosta pack will hunt you—even though you deserve it."

The fuck we won't.

"Because you and I both know that you can't go back home. You were banished to the Dark Court with your father for a reason, and your father wants to secure his crown, so... Earth is the only realm that will accept you. Bring me my payment, and you will have nothing to worry about from our pack."

Her smile turned cold despite the flames that seemed at home on her skin.

"Don't? And I will make sure you never stop running. There will be no safe place to lay your head or rest. No one hiding you, no one making sure you stay alive, no one showing you an ounce of mercy. Understand?"

Tristan's gaze fell from Wren's to Mariella's and back to the woman burning him. The threads of their bond growing brighter. *Gods be damned. They...*

"We will never stop hunting you—not until we take an iron blade to your neck, or worse, our pack brings you to me. Now, do we have a deal?"

The Fae Prince gritted his teeth but gave an emphatic nod.

"The words," Nico growled, knowing full well a Fae or a demon deal required consent. *And if Wren wasn't at least in some part a demon, I'd eat my fucking tie.*

"We have a deal," Tristan gasped. "I will bring back the forty-three women stolen from Earth by my father. If they live, I will bring them home or give you the bones of those that have passed. I will not kill them, deal with them, or cause any undue harm."

"Excellent."

Wren let go of his wrist, the skin not quite as charred as I'd thought it would be. Where her hand had been was a blackened brand of shapes and lines, forming an intricate sigil.

"What did you do to me?" he whispered as his trembling fingers reached for the burn.

Wren's lips tipped up. "Cemented our deal. The marks will go away once you have fulfilled our bargain, and they allow me to track you on any plane should you decide to break it. You will also have a chaperone."

At the snap of her fingers, Wyatt strode forward, cutting the distance with long, purposeful strides that told me he would take great pleasure in Tristan not even attempting to fulfill his deal.

My grip slipped on Fiona, but I caught her. I hadn't known…

Wyatt slapped my brother's shoulder. "Don't worry so much, Nic. You'll grow yourself an ulcer."

Wyatt bent, giving Wren a hug and then petting Ghost. When he straightened, he was kitted out in armor and weapons, a little gift from Wren and the magic bestowed upon her by Zephyr.

"Be right back," he said, striding for the door like a man on a mission. "Come on, Pixie Dust, we've got a job to do."

Tristan stared at the brand on his arm before meeting Wren's still-flaming gaze. "This will go away when I deliver them, yes? No tracking, no hidden spells, I'll just be free."

Wren tipped up her chin. "That's the deal, but I'll offer a word of warning. Should Wyatt not return, or return harmed in any way, we'll strike a brand-new deal —one that will leave your mother gutted in front of you after I cut your eyelids away so you can't even blink. Understand?"

Tristan's face went white as he shakily nodded. "Yes."

"Fabulous. Now, off you go."

And then I watched the Fae I hated walk through the same fucking gate that had ruined everything three years ago.

And I didn't even get breakfast.

16

FIONA

I couldn't recall a single time when I wanted to slap the shit out of my best friend more than I did right then.

Wren had let Tristan go. She had allowed that lousy no-good motherfucker of a Prince just walk back into the Fae realm without even asking the rest of us. The rage that I had kept at bay—*barely*—over the last hour while I dressed in clothes that weren't mine and walked in shoes that weren't mine down to Chatham Square only to find the entire Acosta pack there...

It wasn't fair. She couldn't just do that. She couldn't...

But before I could get out of Theo's hold or march across that blackened square and slap the crap out of her, she snapped her fingers, whisking us back to the pack house as if she were a supernatural taxi service.

My stomach revolted, as did my skin. As good as it felt to be held by Theo, I knew he didn't want to be holding me. Hell, he didn't want anything to do with me. Wasn't that the gist of what was said over bullshit morning-after pancakes?

Nico whisked Wren away, his grip on her bicep like iron, and it wasn't like I could follow Tristan and Wyatt. It didn't make any sense why she would let them go.

"They're getting the prisoners back," Theo said in my ear, his grip softening just a little. "She branded him, made it so he had to get the women the king stole back. I guess there were a bunch in the dungeon where Wren was kept, but she couldn't take them with her."

And while that seemed all hunky-dory, what was keeping him from fucking off into Narnia, never to be seen again?

I must have said that out loud because Theo answered me again. "The brand has a locator in it," he rumbled in my ear, his grip loosening but never falling away. "She'll be able to find him no matter where he is. Plus, Wyatt will make sure he holds up his end of the deal."

I remembered the day we were told just how bad it

could have been for us. Wren and I had been taken by a shady death mage.

Kidnapped.

Stolen.

The mage planned on selling us to the Fae King, but when he'd taken me, he realized he'd nabbed the wrong woman. His buyer had only wanted Wren, and had she not looked for me—had she not ceaselessly scoured the camp—I wouldn't be alive right then.

I owed her everything, and still, I wanted to slap the shit out of her.

Because, of course, she was better than me. Of course, she would want every woman that mage had ever sold to be brought back to safety. This was why she would be a great agent, why she deserved to be an Alpha's mate, and why she should help lead his pack.

Wren wanted to save lives.

I just wanted revenge.

I shrugged off Theo's hold, madder at myself that I wanted it than anything else. If I were being honest, he had a good reason to hate me. He had a reason to hate my father. What my father had stolen from him was a lifetime of happiness. There wasn't a damn thing I could do to replace that.

"I'm fine. It's *fine*." But that didn't stop my chest from feeling like it was going to cave in if I looked at him, and it didn't stop my gut from churning or my eyes stinging, and it didn't abate an ounce of the rage boiling in me.

If what I saw was true, then Wren had branded him with a demon deal. I'd only seen it done once before—the geometric edges of this sigil burned into his skin. There was no breaking that deal, and since he'd accepted it, Tristan would follow through, or he would pay the ultimate price.

Resigned, hurting, and slightly faint since I hadn't actually gotten to eat my breakfast, I made a beeline for the back door, praying no one looked at me funny when I scoured the kitchen for food.

Ignoring Theo—and pretty much anyone else—I slipped in through the back door, the giant lug following me like he was afraid I would cut and run. Or maybe break.

I wasn't going to break.

I had gone through worse than this, had four months of dying slowly, painfully. I could do this, too. I could wait Tristan out—until those women came back—and then I could take an iron spear and jam it right up his ass.

I was my father's daughter, after all, wasn't I? And the Jacobs Coven always got revenge.

And that's what I would always be. A *Jacobs*.

Filling a pilfered plate, I stole five pieces of bacon off a platter in the middle of the kitchen island, with a heaping scoop of eggs, a blueberry muffin, and a glass of orange juice bigger than my face. I had hoped I wouldn't cross paths with anyone, but my luck ran out when I tried to sneak past Catia Acosta.

The Acosta matriarch was three centuries old if she was a day, but she and I appeared around the same age. Several inches taller than I was, she had a gorgeous plait of dark hair hanging in a rope down her back. Devoid of makeup, she was the most naturally beautiful woman I'd ever seen in my life.

"Well, look who's out of the dungeon. I sort of thought you would come and give me a hug when you were finally free."

A wash of guilt filled my belly because Catia had never been anything but lovely to me. But shame did a lot of horrible shit to people. When I was locked down, I didn't want anyone to see me. Now that I was out of the basement, it was easy to see that I had hurt her.

I'd hurt all of them.

"It was a long day yesterday, and so much happened. I'm sorry I didn't come to see you."

The apology felt slightly disingenuous considering what—*or rather who*—I was doing instead. But that information could stay right in my fool brain, never to be uttered again.

"You look all healed up," Catia muttered, squeezing

my shoulders. "The last time I saw you, a skeleton had more meat on its bones." She wrapped an arm around me, guiding me away from my babysitter. "Come to the dining room. Everyone wants to see you."

And all this with Theo at my back, hovering like a nanny. It was tough not to grind my teeth. I kept my mouth shut and followed her, accepting the welcome of the pack while I choked down breakfast. By the time I'd swallowed my last bit of bacon, I was all caught up on what had happened over the previous four months.

Hours later, I was still gabbing with Hannah, Malia, and Theo's sisters when Wren and Nico stumbled in the door. The air was crackling with Wren's magic, something it had done since she'd returned.

Her gaze met mine like she'd been searching for me, the odd green-gold color flashing with power. "I figured it out, but I need your help. I know you've been under a null cell for about four months, but how do you feel about doing a little magic?"

A little magic turned into a Chatham-Square-sized witch circle, enough stun potions to deplete the reserves of every apothecary known to mankind, and a boatload of fear in my gut. For the last twenty-four hours, I had ignored Theo completely, falling head-first into preparation for likely one of the dumbest plans in the known universe.

Then again, we had come up with plenty of batshit crazy plans recently. What was one more? How else would we completely divest the entire city of Savannah of a host of demons? Personally, if I had an in with a Prince of Hell, I probably would have just asked him how to exorcise an entire city's worth of people instead of figuring it out myself.

Then again, Wren didn't trust anybody—especially not Zephyr—so there was that.

Night had fallen by the time we were all settled in Chatham Square. It was almost peaceful, the flames gone and the ground healing. If it weren't for the fact that we'd be calling roughly the entire city here in just a few minutes, it would have been almost pleasant.

And I wish I were exaggerating, but I wasn't. Not really.

Incorporeal demons were a bitch and a half. Each. And there were a fucking lot of them about to be in this square very soon.

Wren paused at the edge of the pavement, staring at all our hard work.

"Oh, come on," Hannah muttered, hip-checking her as she passed. "You faced down a death mage with no power at all. You can do this."

Wren sent her a skeptical side-eye. "That is an oversimplification, and you know it."

Snickering, I also hip-checked her, only where Hannah was trying not to knock her over, I put my whole ass into it. Wren stumbled a little before flicking me on the nose.

The three of us giggled ourselves stupid, a perfect release before shit went down.

"Oh, good," Malia said on a sigh. "Now I don't have to try and trip you or some other such bullshit to get you to settle down. No offense, Wren, but your power makes nuclear reactors look weak."

She winced, shrugging. "Sorry. But never fear. I'll probably blow the whole wad on the exorcisms, and then you can relax. Speaking of relaxing, I was under the impression you'd be doing that instead of this?" She shot me a glare. "You, too. What are y'all doing here?"

I flicked Wren on the tender meat of her arm. "You know better, and how come you didn't ask Hannah that?"

"Because I choose life?" she muttered, flicking me back.

"Damn right she does," Hannah said under her breath, adjusting her weapons. On top of the axes Hannah had strapped to her back, she also had a satchel filled with as many potions as she could carry. Every one of us did, but especially the few of us who couldn't shift.

Nico cut through the blackened square straight to us, his expression one of a determined Alpha. He whispered in Wren's ear. Only then did she nod to signal she was ready.

"Thank you," she murmured, loud enough for my benefit, even though every single wolf could hear her. "Thank you for being here with us, for being willing to fight. For showing up. I appreciate all of you." She cut a smile at Nico's older brother. "Even you, Theo."

He flipped her off, and she blew him a kiss.

"You all embody what family means, and I will be forever grateful you accepted me into yours." Then she walked to the middle of one of the largest witch circles I had ever seen.

Only then did my chanting start.

She had to be careful with this part of the spell. If she used too much power, she wouldn't have enough left to exorcise the demons, but if she used too little, she wouldn't get them all.

It was a delicate balance—a tight rope we were all barely staying on.

Possessed humans filtered through the carefully constructed wards at the perimeter of the square, the spell allowing the possessed in and no one out unless the wards were taken down from the inside. They wandered as if they were sleepwalking, bumping into each other, stumbling over charred earth until they nearly reached the Hell gate.

They waited, docile as lambs, until Wren amassed almost more demons than the square could hold. Then we moved on to phase two of the plan.

Giving the signal, everyone readied their salt bombs while she did the completely asinine task of waking them up. There were too many to do the entire city at once, so batching them seemed like the best option.

Upset murmurings reached a crescendo, the buzz damn near deafening. Both Wren and I shot pleading glances to Nico, and he let out a whistle so loud, dogs on the fucking moon covered their ears.

"Hey, everybody," Wren began. "I know you're confused, but I need you to pay attention."

I gestured to the Hell gate while Wren continued her exit announcements like I was their damn cruise director or something. "This is the Hell gate. We are closing it tonight. If you wish to go home where it is warm, I need you to politely exit your host's body and pass through the gate immediately."

The demon closest to me practically clapped he was so happy. "Thank Deimos and all the torturers in Hell," he said, nearly knocking me over with a feather. "Prince Zephyr told us we needed to stay here until you sent us home, and we cannot *wait* to get out of here. No offense, lady, but this place is freezing. I haven't been this cold since the Cubs won the World Series, and even then, Hell only froze over for twenty minutes, tops. I'm not allowed to kill anyone, I can't eat the animals, and the fresh meat selection is lacking."

Pressing my lips together, I tried to hold in my snicker.

"Umm... no offense taken?"

But reality set in quicker than lightning. Why would Zephyr tell them to stay? Did that mean Wren hadn't needed to amass all this power?

"Did Zephyr say anything else?" Nico asked, his voice low and commanding, making the demon stand up straight. "Give you any other instruction?"

The demon frowned at him before cutting his gaze to Wren and then to me as if he were waiting to see if we were cool with him spilling the beans.

"It's okay. This is my husband and our pack. You can tell us."

"Zephyr said we had to take care of our hosts. Keep them fit and fed and clean. We couldn't destroy their lives in any way—which is rude. These people accepted us of their own free will—putting 'Welcome' signs everywhere. It was as if they were just asking to be possessed, and we couldn't do *anything*. It was actually quite opportune because not all of us could find a host and had to go back home."

Jesus Fucking Christ on a parade float.

"That's not—" Wren looked like she was trying not to explode. "The 'Welcome' signs are meant for humans. Those are not blanket consent. Did anyone express their consent where your host said that you could possess them and not just a 'Welcome' sign? Raise your hands."

A decent pocket of people raised their hands, including the demon closest. Okay, so not a total takeover via cutsie welcome mats.

"But more, Prince Zephyr said that we must obey you. Protect you. He said a battle was coming, and you would need the help."

"Anyone who did not get express consent from your host or gained it using trickery, it is time to leave. Now. Go home to Hell, and thank you for caring for your hosts. Your job is done."

There was one such demon about ten feet away, and she gave us a grave nod before tilting her head back. Then she vomited an oily black smoke into the sky, her whole body shaking like she was being electrocuted. The black smoke headed for the gate, slipping into the seams of the door before winking out of sight.

One down...

The demon's host—a yoga-pants-wearing, mom-bun-having human crumpled to the ground on her hands and knees, coughing up what remained of the black sludge. Then one by one, the others followed suit, blotting out the full moon and all the stars with the incorporeal bodies of the demons on their way home. By the time it was all said and done, we had maybe thirty humans wondering how the fuck they'd gotten here.

That's where I came in. With a wave of my hand, the bright-blue potion bottles surrounding the gathered demons exploded, their contents waving through the air as it sought out the non-possessed like heat-seeking missiles. The smoke collided with the humans, filling their noses, leaving them like mindless automatons.

"Go home, go to bed, remember nothing of this night," I commanded. "You will awake in the morning and go back to your life as you know it."

When I mentioned a potion that could replicate a vampire's compulsion ability, I neglected to tell her just how drugging the effects would be. Those poor humans would be on a twenty-four-hour acid trip from hell. But it was the best I could do.

The group moved in different directions, heading to wherever they called home.

This was good, so why did it feel like it was about to bite us all in the ass?

17

FIONA

"I don't like this," Theo said, moving closer to our circle.

A part of me was glad Theo was so close. The other part never wanted to see his stupid face again.

"Fi, call the rest of the demons," Nico ordered. "Fuck the batching shit. Get them all here. Now."

"On it," I replied, nodding. He was right. "You might want to put out a call to our ABI buddies. Demon-possessed humans aren't exactly the top of the food chain."

Wren jerked her chin in the affirmative before waving her hands in an intricate dance. Cell phone towers had been down since the Hell gate opened, as well as most Internet access. Wren's little hand-waving was the only way to get a long-distance message out.

"She might get wigged out by the mental download," Wren said, shrugging, "but it got the job done."

Then the whole world seemed to tilt. The ground pitched, roiling beneath our feet as all those demons poured right back out of the Hell gate. Blacking out the sky, they screamed past us, shouting warnings that none of us could hear.

The door burst wide as the flames ignited once again, and out came scores of Fae, but none of us were paying attention to the smaller offerings from the Fae realm. They didn't seem to want to be here at all. No, we were looking at the tall man with the bone crown waltzing onto our plane like he had any right to be here.

Desmond.

This was the asshole who'd almost gotten us all killed. Like most Fae, he had a long fall of hair, his the blackest of midnight with the same sharp features his son had. But while his son was tall, Desmond was taller, thinner, and power seemed to roll off him in waves.

Desmond scanned the crowd of shifters and demons and his amassed army of Fae before he landed on Wren. His mouth stretched wide in what could have been a smile, delight hitting his eyes. He'd come for her, and he'd get her over my cold, dead corpse.

"Wren Bannister," the fucker simpered, his smile a touch too big for his face, his sharp white teeth too large for his mouth. "I've been looking for you."

"Funny," Wren shot back, "I was sort of hoping you'd have fallen off a cliff by now and drowned in your own blood." She pulled a sharp dagger from the sheath at her hip as she drew Hannah, Malia, and me to her with her magic, placing us inside the circle. "Looks like neither of us are getting what we want."

Wren stabbed the earth with her blade, and a circle of golden magic drew up from the ground like a shield. "You couldn't touch me there, and you sure as shit can't touch me here. So whatever throne you want, you're not getting it."

Desmond sauntered forward and put a single finger to Wren's ward. His finger sizzled, but he didn't so much as flinch. "I was hoping for more power from you. What with your parentage and demon lineage and all. Pity. But the pack you provided and the demons just lying about? Well, they might just do the trick. I'll even take your husband this time. Had I known you were mated to a Spirit Alpha, I would have had my son steal you both."

Wren ripped the blade out of the earth and threw it,

hitting the Fae right next to Desmond in the neck. This close to the open Fae gates, she'd insisted on using iron blades. Now I could have kissed her for thinking of it because that Fae dropped like a stone, catching Desmond off guard.

"Protect the daughter of Zephyr," the demon closest to Wren cried into the night, and the rest obeyed, surrounding her in a wall of bodies.

Possessed humans didn't have a ton of magic, but they were better than nothing, and the incorporeal ones? Well, they were already wreaking havoc with the Fae around Desmond, choking them, blinding them, doing anything and everything they could to give us an advantage. But it wasn't like I was just going to sit there. My spells, the brute force of Hannah, and the claws and fangs of the Acosta pack...

We gave our all.

But nothing touched Desmond.

Nico jumped before any of us could tell him to stop.

All any of us could do was scream as Desmond's arm shot out, plucking Nico's wolf right out of the air like a flower in a garden before tossing him away like trash.

Wren screamed, casting demons and wolves and Fae alike away as if they had all been pulled by a string. Even I couldn't stay on my feet.

She drew Desmond to her, reaching his ward and digging her fingers in it like she could bend the magic to her will. Desmond's smile—which had seemed so joyous before—trembled and fell.

"You think you can come here to my home and start wrecking shit? You think you can take and take and take and no one will put an end to your fuckery? You think you can hurt my family and I won't put your ass in the ground?"

But as mad as she was, she didn't realize the danger she was in.

"Stop, Wren," I called, but she didn't so much as spare me a glance.

I was using all I had to push against the horde of Fae Desmond had somehow called to us from all around Savannah. But I couldn't get to her. Because she was so focused on ripping away Desmond's protection, she removed the barrier between them.

The glint of the knife had magic exploding out of me, knocking everyone away as I ran for her. He wrapped his fingers around her throat, lifting her to eye level, and I caught sight of her spitting in his face, the blood-tinged saliva painting his skin red.

Then he dropped her.

A flash of red-stained white fur sailed over everyone,

heading straight for Desmond. Ghost bowled over the Fae King, his fangs tearing into his shoulder as the pair of them rolled. Desmond howled in pain as Ghost readjusted his grip, ripping the wound wide and damn near taking the whole arm off. Desmond's uninjured arm shot out, calling the blade that was still in Wren's middle back to him.

Then that blade was in Ghost, tearing him open just like she was. The giant wolf yelped, staggering away as Desmond cradled his abused arm.

But I just couldn't get there. I'd summoned a Prince of Hell before. It was time I called in the big guns. Slamming my magic into the ground, I burned a very special sigil into the charred earth.

Zephyr. Aemon. Bael. I prayed, calling for the three princes. *I call upon you to save your kin. I summon you here and now.*

As if my spell cut through everything, the three demons appeared, hovering over Wren with Nico at their sides. Princes. Brothers.

They were going to help her—them. They were. At the demons' presence, the Fae scattered, reading the writing on the wall. Suddenly, my path was very clear.

"Jesus fucking Christ, Bird. What happened to you?" Nico cradled Wren to his chest. "Not again. Please, no, I can't do this again. Stay with me."

"We're losing them," Zephyr warned, scraping his fingers through her open middle before mixing it with Ghost's blood. "I—we—can help."

"I don't care what it costs," Nico growled, "or what favor you need. Whatever it is, do it. I'm not losing her again."

The two men and Zephyr locked gazes and nodded. Each one dipped their fingers in the blood, drawing a rune with it into the side of their cheeks. Zephyr latched onto Nico.

"Sorry about this. It's gonna hurt."

All three brothers snapped their fingers at once, and Ghost, Nico, and Wren convulsed.

Then Ghost melted into a pool of golden light, his fur, flesh, and blood just gone. That pool of light reached for Wren, coating her body.

When it faded, Wren curled into Nico's arms, and I nearly fell to my knees. Only...

A flash of a bone crown caught my eye, and I *moved.* Slamming magical fire into him, he fell, and Hannah scooped him up by the ankle, his bone crushed in her hand as I continued to bombard him with shit I knew would hurt.

Flesh burned and screaming, he tried to claw away, but not before Malia slammed her heel into his shin bone, snapping it in half. Then she knelt, holding onto his head, her hands glowing as she poured something into him as he tried to bat her away with his one good arm.

"You like pain?" she snarled in his face. "This is all the pain you caused. Fucking choke on it."

Then a midnight-blue, winged, scaled, monster of a wolf stalked toward Desmond. I stumbled back, and a warm hold snatched me up off my feet, setting me behind a familiar broad back. He clutched me to him, not letting me move as Desmond's screams were quickly cut off.

Sweet mother of...

"Was that *Wren*?" I whispered against Theo's back, my fingers gripping his torn and bloody shirt.

He looked at me over his shoulder, giving me a quick nod. And that's when I knew I'd been right. Wren had been dying, and they'd saved her—by any means necessary.

I didn't even know what my friend was anymore, but as long as she was breathing, I didn't care.

At the squelching ripping sounds, my stomach turned, and I was more than happy that Theo had decided to shield me from them. Once upon a time, I had been my father's enforcer, but that didn't mean I enjoyed watching someone get ripped apart. Before I could lose my lunch, Zephyr appeared on my right, startling both me and Theo into stumbling back.

"Once my kin has finished with her meal, I believe you and I have a gate to close."

I couldn't stop myself from rolling my eyes. Had I known it would have been as easy as talking to the Prince of Hell, I would have summoned him earlier.

As if reading my thoughts, he answered, "The events happened in exactly the right order. Fate is a fickle woman. It's best to stick to her plans. Now, the gate?"

My gaze narrowed, and I didn't even try to stop myself from sassing a demon. "No offense, hoss, but I didn't open it on purpose the first time. Unless you have an instruction manual in your pocket, I don't know how to close it."

Zephyr's smile widened, and a tall blond Prince of Hell appeared at his side. This wasn't the first time I'd come across Aemon. He and his wife Darby had paid me a visit what seemed like decades ago, advising me to get out from under my father's thumb. It was Darby's advice that had me joining the ABI.

Unfortunately, her estimation of my goodness was severely lacking.

I met Aemon's chilling gaze, and Theo turned us so I was farther behind him as he stood in between me and the demons. Aemon tilted his head to the side, a bemused smile on his face.

"Shall I tell Darby what you've been up to down here? I'm sure she'd love to hear all about your latest adventure."

Considering our last adventure together, I really wished he wouldn't. Darby Adler was the Warden of Knoxville and a daughter of Death. If there was one person on the planet that I had no intention of pissing off, it was that woman.

"Maybe keep this one between us?" I mean, I had been mostly good, right? Okay, so I was a royal fuck-up of the highest order, but I didn't mean to do it on purpose.

His smile widened, and Theo shifted his weight. "I think if this gate gets closed, she will be more at ease. Good thing you're on our side, right?"

The best I could do was shrug. What else was there to say?

I was not living up to my potential? Shocker.

Zephyr held out a hand, giving Theo a bemused expression when the wolf growled at him. As he guided me toward the accidental doorway, the demon leaned down to whisper in my ear. "Aemon's wife summoned me by accident once. Don't tell her I told you that. She gets testy when you remind her that she fucks up occasionally, too."

I could have sworn I had heard something along those lines on the grapevine ages ago, and damn if they didn't make me feel a little better.

"Now, my little witch. Close your eyes and think about all the demons going home. After you see in your head every demon passing through the gate, I want you to imagine it melting into the ground and the grass and flowers returning to the square."

Reluctantly, I closed my eyes, following his instructions even though they seemed silly. Magic wasn't simply envisioning things. It was mathematics and science wrapped in a power none of us really knew the origins of. It was energy and transference.

But when I opened my eyes again, the thorned gate with its skull head was gone. The grass was indeed green again, and the flowers had bloomed even at midnight. It was as if I had never opened the gate at all, except Zephyr remained.

"See? I knew you could do it. You really should listen to me more."

I snorted. "Yes, anytime I need a demon consult, I'll be sure to contact you."

He gave me a cheeky smirk before striding over to a human-shaped Wren and dropping a kiss on her temple. Then he and his two brothers winked out of sight.

I wanted to feel relief—wanted to feel something, anything—but all I got was numbness.

Which was probably why when Theo tucked me under his arm and guided me away, I didn't protest. And when he led me into his house and peeled off my clothes, I let myself feel good for the first time all day.

But I knew it couldn't last.

And it didn't.

18

THEO

The first good night of sleep I got in years had been with Fiona in my arms. Personally, I thought it was a fluke. We had just scratched an itch that had been building for months, and I was content. Of course I would sleep great. I wasn't on a stupid metal folding chair in a dank dungeon but in my own bed and so satisfied I could believe that was what happiness was actually like.

But now that I'd had her twice, I knew it wasn't my bed.

It was Fiona.

I could barely make myself leave her the first

morning. All I'd wanted to do was see her eat a full meal without getting sick. Then everything went to shit.

Not wanting a repeat of that fiasco, I stayed in this bed and prayed that when she woke up, she didn't rethink being in it with me. Sifting my fingers through purple hair, I remembered how fucking scared I was the night before. Wren had assumed Fiona would sit the battle out—bow out of a fight that could kill us all.

I knew different.

Fiona fought fiercely for the people that she loved, and she loved my pack. When we had taken them in after Wren was stolen, Fiona had made it her mission to get to know everyone—to help where she could. She fortified the warding, helped Nico find his wife. And what had I done?

I'd shunned her just like every other new pack member over the last decade.

But that didn't stop her from giving nearly everything she had. Last night I was supposed to protect my brother, was supposed to protect his wife. Instead, I found myself ripping Fae apart one by one. Anyone who came too close to Fiona met the end of my claws.

Fiona didn't get touched—not once—because I made it so.

Shame warred with satisfaction in my gut. I didn't deserve to be Nico's second because I hadn't protected him one bit. I had turned my back on my Alpha to save the woman in my arms, and the worst part of it all?

I didn't regret it.

That's the part that's stuck for me. I didn't regret not saving him. I didn't regret not helping him because the woman in my arms was safe and alive and whole.

The funny part? A year ago, I could have sworn I hated her. If someone had asked me what I thought about Fiona before we were stuck together in that dungeon, I would have said she was a shady Jacobs plant out to steal Savannah for herself.

Now I knew the woman in my arms would rather cut off her own hand than hurt my family.

So I stayed put, not moving, barely breathing, letting this beautiful woman use me as a pillow for fear that she would come to her senses and leave me in her dust.

The fragile peace was broken when Fiona ripped herself from my arms and shot out of bed like her ass was on fire. Don't get me wrong, I enjoyed the show, but I was looking around for the threat in the room while she scrambled to shove her feet in her underwear and slap a bra on her chest.

"Leaving so soon? Trying to avoid another breakfast fiasco, I take it?" I pillowed my head on my arms as she froze like a deer in headlights.

She blinked at me, her gaze moving around the room

before falling on my face again. It was like she was coming back to herself, and I realized just how bad being cooped up in that cell had damaged her. She was whole again physically, but mentally it would take more than a few days to remind her that she wasn't being hunted anymore.

"Desmond is dead, right? The Hell gate is closed. The Fae gates are open." She blinked hard, her shoulders drooping in relief. "Desmond is dead. Wren... she's alive. Everybody's alive. We didn't lose anyone, right?"

She sucked in a breath and let it out while she shuddered with adrenaline overload.

"I'm not dreaming. That—that's what happened, right?"

I wanted to go to her, to hold her, if only for a little while, but I didn't want to scare her off. Instead, I sat up, focusing on her.

"You're right. The demons are gone. Zephyr left. Everything's back to rights."

Fiona's chest heaved, her eyes skittering around the room like she expected a threat to jump out at her.

"What's going on, Cupcake? You seem mighty upset for somebody who won last night."

Her gaze stopped its incessant scanning to fall at her feet. She shook her head, clutching her discarded shirt to her belly as she shifted from foot to foot. "Do you—do you think the ABI will keep looking for me? Do you think that they will buy the story we sell? Is everything going to go back to the way it was before?"

I supposed that depended on what she meant by "before."

If she meant the city of Savannah, her ABI career, her relationship with Wren, then probably. She could likely return to being a good little agent living in Savannah and starting her life away from her family.

If she meant us, then the answer was most definitely no. I didn't think I could go back to hating her or wishing that she would go away, or blaming her for the sins of her father. I couldn't go back to her being a stranger.

But telling her that was most definitely out of the question.

"I'm not sure," I murmured, choosing honesty. "I'm not exactly certain they were ever really looking for you in the first place. The ABI was looking for a magical signature—not a person. Do you still think you have the dark magic inside you? Or did you use it all?"

Fiona had killed twelve witches for their power—a dark power that poisoned her. Opening that gate had nearly killed her, but had she not, my pack would have never healed. In theory, the opening should have used all that magic up, and the null cell detoxed the rest.

But whether or not she had the stain of that magic anymore was up for debate.

She shook her head, fisting the shirt at her belly. "I don't know. I worry that a part of it will always be in me. That I'll always have the mark of it on my soul. That if I step one foot in that building, they're going to look at me and just know."

Fiona began to pace, unable to look at me for more than a second. "Problem is? I would do it again. We got her back. We beat them. I should feel good about what I did. I took evil men off the streets. I saved my friend. But I still feel guilty—still feel the evilness inside me. Still… Under the null wards, I could almost pretend like I had done a good thing. But now that I'm free? I feel more in danger than I ever did when I was actually dying."

That got me off the bed. Prowling toward her, I snatched the shirt from her hands, backing her up against the closest wall. I would have loved to say this was for effect, but it was mostly so I could corral her close to me and feel her skin against mine. Lifting her off her feet, I brought her to eye level so I could stare at that pretty face and tell her just how wrong she was.

"You have a horrible habit of second-guessing yourself, Cupcake. I'm going to need you to quit it. You saved the day. You kept Desmond from escaping. You closed the Hell gate."

Flexing my fingers, I jostled her until she wrapped her arms around my neck and her legs around my back.

"You summoned all those demons back home. You did that. Wren had to amass an insane amount of power for a fraction of the city. You did the rest. You took out so many threats on that battlefield."

Enough to scare the shit out of me and probably take a century off my life.

"You made it so we could be free again, and you're worried about twelve witches who shouldn't have been allowed to live in the first place. Getting your hands dirty is the price we pay for protecting the pack."

Fiona's lip trembled, but she met my eyes. "So I'm not completely evil then?"

I fought off the urge to spank her ass. "You know better than the rest of us that everyone has shades of grey. Some of those shades might be a little darker than others, but we all have light in us, too."

"I just thought I could be better, you know? That if I got away from my family, I could be a better person. I could be a rule-follower, but the rules cage people like me. They make it so the bad guys get away more often than not, and good people get hurt. I wanted to make a difference, but I don't know if I can be an agent anymore."

Walking backward, I found the bed and sat with her

on my lap, bumping her ass so we tumbled, and she was lying across my chest like we'd started the day.

"Why don't you worry about the meaning of life when you have a full belly and haven't just survived three years of bullshit, yeah?"

She pursed her lips. "So, you're saying maybe I should settle down a little bit?"

"Nooooo," I whispered, knowing damn well how close that sounded to a "calm down." I might not have learned too much in my decades on this planet, but telling a woman to calm down was at the tippy top of the things that I had.

She narrowed her eyes. "Fine. I'll settle down."

"And eat some food."

She giggled. "And eat some food."

The ring of a cell phone startled us both. Frowning, she sat up, her eyes catching on the powder-blue duffel Hannah delivered last night. The nearly seven-foot-tall ghoul had given me a piercing look that told me she would eat my arm off if I hurt Fiona. However, she simply said she didn't want to make another morning-after clothes delivery.

I would have preferred Fiona without access to clothes or a phone and preferably tied to my bed so she couldn't escape. Unfortunately, that qualified as kidnapping and was frowned upon.

Fiona slid off the bed and stared at the slim device. I knew for a fact that she hadn't used it in months. Fates knew how many missed calls and messages she had, but then again, once the ABI had shut down the city, the cell phone service had taken a hit.

"It's my dad," she mumbled, staring at her phone like it was a snake.

"You don't have to answer it if you don't want to." But the calmness in my voice barely hid my desire to smash that cell to bits.

Josiah Jacobs had no business calling his daughter. He had no reason to fit into her life. As far as he knew, she was an ABI agent in good standing, and he was a mob boss monster disguised as a coven leader.

"Yes, I do. If I don't, he'll come here." She looked up from her phone to spear me with an expression so fearful it brought me to my feet. "I don't want him to come here."

Swallowing, I held out a hand, lending her support as she answered the phone.

"Hello?" One would think Fiona was the picture of calm collectedness—even though two seconds ago she was ready to come out of her skin.

"Thank the Fates, child," Josiah's voice rang down the line, and if I didn't know better, I would think he actually gave a shit about his daughter. "I've been calling for months now. I thought you'd get a message to me or something to say that you were okay, baby girl. You worried us sick. Word is, the ABI just dropped the wards around Savannah. That demons were running around. I know you're busy, kiddo, but I thought—"

"Daddy, you know I would have gotten a message to you if I could," Fiona said, cutting him off. "I'm sorry I worried you, but I was in the trenches over here. It's good to hear your voice. How have you and Mama been?"

Her voice and tone said all the right things, but her face told a vastly different story.

"Oh, well, we've been fine. Things have been real tense over here with all of us worried about y'all. You know your mama's birthday is tomorrow, and we've been discussing throwing her a big ole party. Now that the city is safe again, we'd love to see you."

Fiona's face paled like she'd pass out at any second. I was trying to keep my hold on her hand gentle, so I didn't accidentally crush it.

"Oh, Daddy, I don't know if I'm going to be able to make it on such short notice. The ABI needs me here. Just because the demons are gone doesn't mean everything is back to rights. Please give Mama my best, but no, I can't be there."

He paused for a few beats, the silence stretching on. "Are you sure, Princess?" It was as if the person on the line changed to someone else, even though the voice was the same. "Because I would have thought you'd love to come home. Especially considering the spell you used to gain all that power, Pumpkin. You know, I'm pretty sure I saw a spell just like it in one of your grandmama's grimoires. She was an interesting lady, your grandmamma. She had books filled with all kinds of dark things that probably should never be done. Sort of like a spell to kill a coven's worth of witches. I wonder if your boss knows about that spell, do you think?"

If Fiona had been pale before, she was positively grey then. Before she passed out, I picked her up and sat her on the bed, switching places with her as I began to pace the room. Josiah wanted her home, that was for damn sure. But I knew he wouldn't let her leave once she got there, and I knew he'd lord that spell over her head until he got whatever the fuck it was he wanted.

"I'm sure my boss knows all about spells like that, Daddy. And I'm also sure that I've never read one of Grandmama's books, nor have I ever done a spell like that. Didn't you say all those years ago that killing our own kind was a sin? An act never to be forgiven."

Oh, that was rich coming from that man. Josiah Jacobs had probably killed more witches than he'd saved. He'd probably killed more witches than were in his entire coven. He'd murdered entire families just to keep power. I knew that for certain.

"Come home," he ordered. "Your mother needs you here for her birthday, and then I'll send you back—no muss, no fuss. Won't even be a weekend. Don't make me ask again. I'll send the plane for you. It'll be at the private hangar in three hours. You'd better be on it."

With that final threat, Josiah hung up on his daughter.

I couldn't tell her that she couldn't go. She and I both knew what her father was capable of. Not going was tantamount to a death sentence—especially if he'd rat out his own daughter.

"You're not going by yourself," I said, knowing damn well I shouldn't be within a mile of Josiah Jacobs.

Fiona blinked, sputtered, and slid off the bed to face me.

"Absolutely not. You are not coming with me." She flapped her arms like I was the dumbest idiot she'd ever met. "There is no way I would put you through that torture. You know you can't kill him, right? If you came with me, you wouldn't be able to murder him." Chewing on a forest-green nail, she began to pace. "He has an entire coven at his disposal and his finger in enough pies to bring down the weight of the world on you if you even so much as sneezed at him wrong. No, you can't come."

She paused her pacing, shaking her head, with an unwavering determination laced in her words. No."

"I'm not going to let him hurt somebody else that I care about," I growled, catching her arm as she turned to make another pass. Cupping her chin, I made her look at me. "In case you weren't aware, that includes you. So I'm fucking coming, you got it?"

Worry etched its way across her beautiful face, and I watched in wonder as she packed it away, shoved it down, swallowed it. By the time she was done, her mask was firmly in place.

But mask or not, I knew my Fiona was still in there.

And I wouldn't let her go alone into the lion's den.

FIONA

I knew things were bad when it was Paul that was waiting for us at the private airport outside of my father's compound. His face was like stone as he watched Theo put our bags in the back of the SUV and open the door for me like a doting lover. That wasn't to say that Theo touched me once because he didn't other than holding my hand on takeoff and landing. Theo did his best to display an air of calm indifference when it came to me.

Too bad for him, I knew better.

Paul met my gaze through the rearview mirror of the SUV, unsure of whether or not he should tell me what was really going on. It wasn't like I could read his mind—

I'd just known Paul my whole damn life, and the expression on his face did not spell good things. But knowing how little Paul trusted anyone, he kept his mouth shut, the car ride incredibly silent as we pulled up to the house.

My father's compound was basically the size of a small city tucked away on the Kentucky side of the border of Tennessee. It spanned more acres than I cared to count, filled with every coven member and a fair number of bodies. My father had the house specialty built with warding in every single strut and support, in every brick, and even in the damn mortar.

Nothing short of a nuke could take down this place.

It was stupid to come here. This was a place of power for my father—which was likely why he held meetings here, hosted parties here. Because if someone wanted him dead, they sure as shit wouldn't be able to do it in this house.

Catering trucks and florist vans were parked at the servants' entrance. People scurried in and out carrying flower arrangements and stemware cases, buzzing like bees to get ready for a party I didn't want to attend.

"I hope you got a spell in your back pocket. Your mama is gonna shit a kitten when she sees purple hair," Paul muttered as I got out.

Just touching a toe on this property nearly stole all

the air from my lungs. Still, my smile was positively wicked, belaying my fear. "That's the idea. Purple hair and bringing a wolf with me. Next thing you know, I'm going to get a tattoo and really piss them off."

Paul shook his head. "He wants to meet with you before the party. He's in the study, but be careful. He's been in a mood lately."

"Fantastic," I grumbled, rolling my eyes. "Come on, Theo. Let's meet dear, old dad."

Paul lurched forward, putting a quelling hand on my shoulder only to snatch it back at Theo's menacing growl. Instantly, he put his hands up. "Look, man, I'm just trying to look out for her. She waltzes in there with a wolf, and I don't know what he'll do."

Theo's gaze remained on Paul's raised hand like he'd really enjoy ripping it from his body. "Fiona is a blooded member of the Acosta pack. I am the Alpha's second, and her protection no matter where she goes. If she is to meet with her father, I will go with her, and if you touch her again, you will lose that hand. Are we clear?"

Paul's face went white. "I wasn't aware that's how wolves did things. The pack here doesn't accept witches."

Theo's lip curled in disgust—even though he himself had hated witches once upon a time. "Fiona is the best friend of the Alpha's wife, who is a witch. We make exceptions—especially considering that she has saved the

Alpha's wife not once but twice. As a venerated member of our pack, she goes nowhere in another pack's territory without protection—not even to her father's office. You got me?"

Paul's gaze shifted from me to Theo and back again, realization dawning on his face. Yeah, I never thought we could fool Paul for very long. The story we'd concocted on the plane to explain why Theo had joined me was about the best we could come up with on short notice. The last thing I needed was my parents shitting a litter of kittens because I was in a pseudo-relationship with a shifter.

Not that I'd call Theo and I occasionally hate-fucking each other a relationship, but whatever.

"If that's how you plan on playing it," Paul said, moving to the trunk. "I'll make sure he's set up in the room next to yours."

With that, I guided Theo through the house around scurrying people trying to set up for the party. On the second floor, past the grand staircase, was a giant library, and connected to it was my father's office. I didn't know what it was about heads of families and offices like these. Nico's father had a similar one, though I doubted it had as many grimoires as ours did. Gathering myself, I knocked on the door, trying not to lose my nerve.

I needed to be the version of myself my father was used to. The calm, cool, and collected enforcer he'd made

—or rather, *wanted* me—to be. I was supposed to be put together and coy and as sweet as sugar.

Too bad I didn't know that girl anymore.

"Come in," my father called, and I shot Theo a look over my shoulder before opening the door and walking in. My father sat behind a broad mahogany desk, the sprawling thing barely occupying a small fraction of the room.

Josiah Jacobs was the formidable man I'd always known him to be. With salt-and-pepper hair—heavy on the pepper—he could pass for forty-five if he was a day. Tall and tan, he was my opposite in almost every way. But I was looking at him through a new lens. I'd never believed people when they told me who he was. I'd always assumed my father had done despicable things to stay in power but that they had been necessary. But I hadn't quite realized what he had done to the witches in our community—to the families he'd slaughtered.

My father had always taught me it was us or them, that they would kill us the first chance they got. That they would take everything from us, that the community would be better with him in power.

Theo would live out his days without a mate because of my father, and it didn't matter how much he might like me, that would always be a sticking point, wouldn't it?

"My darling girl. I'm so glad you made it," Dad said as he stood from his chair, engulfing me in a hug that was just a touch too hard. "And who is this strapping fellow?"

"Dad," I croaked before clearing my throat, "this is Theo Acosta, the second of the Acosta pack. For all intents and purposes, he is my bodyguard while I'm in another pack's territory. Theo, this is my father, Josiah Jacobs."

Theo inclined his head but said nothing. If I didn't know any better, I would assume he was just a stoic guard, and not trying to avoid murdering my father in his own home.

But I did know better.

"Wow, making contacts and moving up the ranks. It's good to see your pack is so interested in my daughter's safety. I appreciate you coming out to make sure there aren't any hiccups with her visit. But if you'll excuse us, I would like to talk to my daughter in private."

Theo's lips tipped up in what could have been chagrin. "I'm afraid I am to be within sight of Miss Jacobs at all times while she is in another pack's territory. My Alpha was very clear, and I cannot disobey him. You understand."

Even I heard my father's teeth grind, and I didn't have Theo's ears.

"Very well," he said, and if I were anyone else, I

would assume his acquiescence was as good-natured as he pretended it to be. But I knew the malice in his tone when I heard it, and if Theo didn't play his cards right, neither of us would be making it out of here.

"I suppose you should get ready for the party, then," he said, twirling a lock of my purple hair around his finger before letting it go. "I'm sure your mother will want to see you before the party starts."

Swallowing, I gave him my best sugary-sweet smile. "Of course. I'll get settled in my room. It was very good to see you, Dad," I lied woodenly, thankful to pull away from him.

Somehow, I got us out of that office and to my room without incident. I didn't bother going to find my mother. Belladonna Jacobs was not like Catia Acosta. If I knew my mother, she was likely in the middle of one of her beauty rituals. Hell, she was probably sacrificing a fucking goat or something to try and reduce her fine lines. Unless my mother was criticizing me, I seriously doubted she gave a ripe shit about seeing me at all.

I hadn't seen either of my parents in the three years Wren had been missing, avoiding going home as much as humanly possible. It was easy to use the ABI as an excuse. My father hated them and everything they stood for. He hated many things concerning the law but especially the people who enforced it. Unless he could buy them off, that was.

After I'd been taken at selection school, he'd actually thought I would quit and return home. I'd had to talk circles around that man just to get everything set up in Savannah. I didn't know what he would have done if Paul hadn't been there to talk him down. The only saving grace for the selection school was that Nico had killed that death mage.

I didn't want to be here, and if there had been another way around it, I wouldn't be. I just had to find out what my father wanted and get the hell out before I got stuck here.

By the time the party was underway, my nerves were all but fried. Theo, to his credit, was far calmer than I was. I couldn't say what it was for sure, but the way my father insisted on me coming here—objecting to an excuse I'd used for years—set my teeth on edge. Something was wrong, and I knew this party would set it off.

Decked out in a dress my mother would approve of, I did my best to return to the girl I used to be and not fidget all over the place. The floor-length gown was flesh-toned at the bodice, encrusted with iridescent crystals, the fabric fading to a vibrant pinky-purple color that matched my hair. It was held up by two skinny straps, and the back was practically nonexistent. And I so enjoyed the heat in Theo's gaze when he saw me in it.

My mother didn't do anything less than black tie, so I was incredibly pleased to find Theo in a sharp designer tuxedo and a purple pocket square. If I didn't know any better, I would think he chose that color on purpose to match my dress.

Guests in their finery milled about, their discussions like little buzzing bees in the background. Years ago, I would have introduced myself to them, listen in on their conversations, or glean new information for my father. Sometimes I'd even spell people in this very house, making sure they did what my father wanted. I was his not-so-secret weapon because so few of them ever suspected that my dad would use someone like me to do his bidding.

No one suspects the badger. They always suspect the snake. That was his favorite saying, and he was right.

Theo followed a few paces behind me as I made my way into the ballroom, ready to get this night over with. As soon as I entered, I felt the shift of the crowd. Everyone around me started clapping, much to my confusion. Gently, Theo guided me through the revelers toward my parents. I almost didn't see any of it, a part of me wishing Theo would pick me up and whisk me out of there.

When I made it to my father, it was clear that this party was not for my mother's birthday. All I had to do was wait for him to drop the bomb. When he held his arm out to bring me closer, I fought the urge to back away, allowing him to draw me in and steal the microphone from the crooning singer serenading us all.

"Now that the guest of honor has arrived, please give her a round of applause," my father bellowed through the microphone to the titters of the crowd.

My mother hugged me as well, pressing a ruby-red kiss to my cheek before she waved her fingers to wipe it away.

"Congratulations, Sweetheart," she whispered in my ear, but I had no idea what she was congratulating me on.

"It pleases me to no end," my father continued, "that my only daughter Fiona has returned to us. And to strengthen the alliance between our two covens, she has accepted the proposal of Hendrick Lane. Let us all rejoice in their engagement."

Was I hallucinating, or did my father just tell this whole room full of witches that I was engaged to my ex-boyfriend? Swallowing hard, a ringing filled my ears, drowning out the murmurs and congratulations of the crowd. I backed up out of my father's hold, staring at him like I'd never seen him before in my life.

If this was what he neglected to tell me, he should have tried harder than springing this on me with no fucking warning. A part of me wished I had claws like Theo. Maybe some talons. I'd rip him in two right there and then.

Hendrick Lane stood on the other side of my mother, his smug smile stretching across his face like he'd actually fucking won something. Tall and relatively good-looking, Henrick was the picture of how fast the boarding school to frat bro pipeline could melt someone's brain.

Beside him were his odious parents, the pair pinched but preening at the applause. I hadn't seen any of them in years—not after we ended things. Or rather, I had ended things much to his ire. Hendrick was a user, a parasite. He only wanted power. At first, he was really good at hiding it, but his mask slipped the longer we dated until it was too much for me to ignore.

The Lane Coven wasn't quite as powerful as ours, but they had plenty of ABI connections and a few members on the Council. They didn't have the land or the numbers that we did, but they had influence.

And all this tallied in my brain, adding up to the sum total of exactly what was going on. The only reason to use me as a bargaining chip was if Dad's hold on the region was slipping.

He was selling me for influence.

Rage boiled in my gut, and I decided then and there that I'd rather take a beheading from the ABI for doing what was right than be sold off to this limp-dick asshole for the rest of my life. What was this, the 1800s?

"Absolutely fucking not," I growled loud enough that the people around us stopped clapping and gasped. Three years ago, I would have given a shit. Right then, I really fucking didn't.

"There is no way on this earth or any other that I am marrying that shit stain of a man. I broke up with him for a reason. The primary being, he can't keep his dick in his pants."

Yes, I was shouting, and no, I did not give a fuck. I didn't care about my father's hold on the region, and I sure as shit didn't give two fucks if he thought he was going to tattle on me. The look on my face must have said as much because my father's coloring went as purple as my hair.

My gaze fell on my mother. "Happy fucking birthday, Mom. Nice to see you. I'm out."

Only then did I march right back out of the ballroom, the only sound the click of my high heels.

When the door closed, I fought off the urge to scream. Finding a quiet nook away from everyone took some doing, but eventually, I found one. Fingers sparking, I had a tough time holding onto my magic and not rocking the whole damn house. Finding a bench, I plopped onto it, sliding off my heels in favor of pacing barefoot.

I heard the footsteps before I saw him, and I was about to hug the man I was dying to see until he rounded the corner. Then I realized it wasn't Theo who'd followed me.

It was Hendrick.

His perfectly coiffed and expertly highlighted blond hair was such a contrast to the man I wanted that it made me physically ill. I didn't fear Hendrick. I had more power than he did and far fewer scruples. But I should have.

I was expecting a harsh word or an argument. What I wasn't expecting was the open-handed slap that cracked across my cheek and split my lip. He roughly grabbed my wrist, yanking me to him before I even caught my bearings.

"You stupid bitch. Where the fuck do you get off embarrassing me like that? Do you have any idea how much your father begged to get this engagement in the books? Do you know what he promised us? And you're over here trying to tell me no? You don't get to tell me no."

Trying to wrench my arm from his hold, I slammed a spell right at his feet, making him back up.

Unfortunately, he took me with him. "I didn't agree to anything, so I don't give a shit what my father said."

"Wanna bet?" he hissed, a ball of green fire lighting his palm ablaze. "If you think you're getting out of this deal, you're out of your mind. That badge isn't going to help shit. We own you."

I didn't feel even a little bad when I raked my nails across his cheek, splitting the skin wide. He wanted to act like a fucking animal? I'd treat him like one. Two seconds later, Hendrick was on his ass on the tile floor, nursing a broken nose and some busted balls.

Then I wiped the blood from my mouth, shaking, I was so mad.

"You don't ever touch me again. I don't care what my father promised you or your family. He lied because I'll marry you over my dead body."

Then again, *his* dead body was looking mighty good right about then.

THEO

I had fucked up in a variety of ways in my lifetime. Living as long as wolves did, collecting mistakes and missteps throughout one's tenure on this earth was easy. It was easy to look back and wish to change things you'd done.

Wish for a different outcome.

Wonder if you had changed just one thing, things would have turned out different.

Right then, the only thing I would change was that I would have never let Fiona get on that plane in the first place. Okay, that was total bullshit. I probably would have told Nico where we were going first if we got on the plane at all.

It was a toss-up.

The ballroom of the coven house was done up in bountiful sprays of flowers and elegant lights. People ate from tiny plates filled with classy appetizers and sipped from crystal flutes. It was ostentatious and pretentious and a solid waste of money. My pack had more money than we could ever spend in a hundred lifetimes. Living forever made the accumulation of wealth reasonably simple, but typically we didn't spend it this way.

We didn't waste it.

Not like this.

The story we'd devised to explain away my presence here was only half a lie. We were in another pack's territory. And while the LeBlanc pack wasn't nearly as bloodthirsty as they had been, stepping one toe off that airplane was probably a horrible decision. Still, I wasn't going to leave Fiona to the whims of her father. After that phone call, there was no way in hell she would ever come here alone.

The trouble was as soon as we walked into that ballroom, I failed in the task of staying with her. Eight guards stood in my way as Fiona marched through the crowd to a sea of applause. Not wanting to cause a scene, I didn't struggle too much, skirting around the ballroom so I could keep an eye on her.

But she was just out of reach—too far away for me to

do anything should this party turn into a funeral.

And when her father tucked her under his arm, I fought off the urge to rip it right off him. Fought off the urge to tear into him with my claws and teeth. My wolf roiled under my skin, his silence over the last few days irking me in a way I couldn't pinpoint. My wolf didn't talk as loudly as Nico's did to him, but he was always there.

Pacing.

Waiting.

Watching.

It was possible that my wolf was far more silent because I was eighty-some-odd years older. I'd had time to fully bond, to share a brain, to share space. We were always two separate beings, but over time, we had become as one as we could have been.

But in this room with so many predators in pretty suits and fancy dresses, my wolf was on high alert.

Fully cognizant.

Fully separate.

And ready to take over should the need arise.

The words "welcome," and "proposal," and "engagement" filtered into my brain before a loud buzzing filled my ears, and my chest threatened to cave in on itself. The only thing that kept me sane was Fiona's face.

The shock.

The betrayal.

She hadn't known what was coming.

I barely examined the pompous fuck who her father had promised her to. The sneer on his face told me everything I needed to know. To him, Fiona was a possession. A status symbol. A rung on the ladder. She wasn't a person to him—she wasn't an amazing creature filled with wonder and light and wrath. She wasn't something to be feared and worshipped to him. She was nothing but a stepping stone, and that made me want to rip him apart.

I wanted to rip them all apart—her father for selling her over, her wannabe betrothed, and even her fucking mother who stood there beaming like her daughter was winning a gods-damned beauty pageant.

Fiona stumbled away, her eyes sparking full of magic and fire, her cheeks and chest flushed. That spirit in her that I found so fucking sexy, and then she'd told them all to fuck off. I'd never been so proud. And when she stormed out of the ballroom, I realized this was our cue.

We would have to make a hasty exit because there was no way Fiona's outburst wouldn't be met with absolute consequences.

I moved to follow her but was stopped by Josiah Jacobs himself. That motherfucker had the gall to clamp his hand on my shoulder like I wouldn't rip it from him and make him fucking eat it. I stared at his hand, contemplating whether it would be worth it or not.

"Theo, is it?" her father asked like he didn't know my fucking name. "Why don't we let my daughter cool off a little bit?"

I plucked that hand off my shoulder, not giving in to the urge to crush it. "I'm afraid I can't do that. Fiona is to stay in my sight at all times, and I'm falling down on the job. If you'll excuse me."

Look at me being all sensible and shit.

Fiona had said I couldn't kill him, but the energy coming off the very walls of this place told me the reason why. I highly doubted I could harm Josiah Jacobs in this house.

Pity.

He sidestepped me, getting right in my way as a throng of cronies backed him up. But what Josiah didn't know was that none of these men were particularly loyal to him. Each one would betray him for enough money, enough power, or if they thought someone bigger or better could be in charge. They didn't give a shit about their coven leader, and based on their low-level power, I highly doubted they could give me so much as a paper cut.

Meeting Josiah's gaze, I gave him a snide smile as I

leaned in, taking his scent into my nose, making sure it was imprinted on my brain. "They won't back you up against me or against my pack. Somehow, I think you know this," I murmured, my threat calm as could be. "Not one of them are loyal to you—have never been. Each one would turn their back on you in a heartbeat. So if you want to dance, I'm game. Just know that when I put you on your ass, they're going to find a new master to serve." Pulling away, I allowed my wolf to shine out of my eyes. "Now, can I get back to protecting your daughter, or will I have to teach you a lesson?"

He covered it pretty well, but I still smelled the fear. Josiah Jacobs never had someone stand up to him that he couldn't kill, and he was seriously contemplating how easy or how difficult it would be to end me. But he didn't have the resources for war. That was the reason he was selling his daughter off. Had to be. And he didn't want to war with a wolf—especially not this one.

Because he knew I didn't care about his money or his titles or his reach. I cared about Fiona, and that was it.

When I stepped to the side again, he didn't follow me.

I weaved through the crowd out of the ballroom, trying to track the tenuous scent of Fiona's perfume. The trail was faint, but I still found her. Huddled in a corner in a small alcove in the far east wing, away from most of the guests, she'd slipped off her heels, drawn up her legs, and hugged them to her chest. Her dress billowed out in a cloud around her.

I wished I could have said that it was her beauty that caught my eye first. But my gaze laser-locked on the blooming purple bruises at her wrist. On the bloody cut on her lip.

I thought I knew rage before. I thought I understood what true anger was. But until I felt the fangs in my mouth grow, and the talons erupt from my fingernails, and the wolf howling in my brain, did I truly understand fury.

"Who did this to you?" I growled, barely able to string that single sentence together.

Fiona's cornflower-blue eyes were filled with her own fury and a fair amount of fear. "I handled it. I don't need your help on this one."

"Who did it, Cupcake?" My words were barely above a whisper as I practically vibrated out of my skin.

She wiped at her lip, wincing as she made contact with the cut. "It's fine. I'm *fine*. I just want to get—"

"If you won't tell me his name," I warned, refusing to let this go, "I will find him myself."

As gently as I could, I knelt at her feet, plucking her hand from around her knees, and brought the bruised and delicate wrist to my nose, scenting the motherfucker who put his hands on her.

I had half a mind to let my wolf go free. His nose was better, but mine would do just fine. I followed the stench to the opposite end of the house, where I assumed the guest quarters were located. It made sense in a sort of witchy way. Guests coming in from the west was a sign of good tidings. Too bad, in this case, it was in no way accurate.

"Theo, stop," Fiona urged, her hold on my arm tight. "I handled it."

But she hadn't. Unless that motherfucker was dead, she hadn't handled shit.

Gently, carefully, I cupped her cheeks in my hands. "No one touches you. No one hurts you."

"But—"

Her protests were weak in my ears, and they fell away completely when I kicked in the door to the guest suite.

I was three steps into the room when that pompous fuck-wad she'd been promised to waltzed out of the bathroom, a bloody washrag to his cheek. I didn't wait. I launched myself across that room, fangs and talons at the ready.

Before I could make contact, a ball of fire sailed into my chest, slamming me across the room and into the wall. My wolf took over then, and I lost myself to the grey liminal space of the change as he jumped from my skin, and I was riding shotgun and his brain for a change.

Hendrick froze at the sound of our growl, his pasty skin losing all color as he tried and failed to form another ball of magic in his hand.

Weak. Too weak for our woman. Our Fiona.

On that, my wolf and I wholeheartedly agreed. Once again, I launched myself across the room, my fangs latching into the skin of his shoulder and ripping him to the ground. His blood filled our mouth, but what I wanted to do was crush the hand that had hurt her.

In the span of a single moment, I phased back to two legs, gripped his hand in mine, and crushed every single bone he had in his arm. His howl of agony was music to my fucking ears. Hendrick sputtered pleas of mercy, begging for his own life, but there wasn't a chance I'd let him hurt Fiona again.

There wasn't a chance I'd let myself fail to protect her a second time.

And when he began to gurgle out a curse, I fit my talons against his throat and ripped it out. I watched with glee as the light in his eyes died, as he choked out his last breath.

Straightening, I found Fiona, her back against the wall, a shaking hand covering her mouth. She shoved at my shoulder, but I still picked her up and crushed my lips to hers.

Hungrily, she kissed me, her tongue sweeping into

my mouth, dueling with mine as her fingers fisted into my jacket, pulling me closer.

"Why did you do that? I had it handled. Why did you do that?" she asked when the kiss broke, her breaths coming in ragged pants.

"I told you. No one hurts you. No one touches you. You're mine, understand?" Possessive, protective, it didn't change a thing. "You are mine. No one else's. Mine."

If I wasn't ever going to get a mate chosen for me, I'd choose one for myself. Fiona was it. Her fire, her passion, her loyalty, her protectiveness. As much as I had hated her when we first met, I was falling just as hard for her now.

Fiona nodded, nipping at my lips, reaching for my belt, yanking my shirt, unzipping my pants. We were mindless—aching, needing each other. More than we needed safety, more than we needed air.

A few moments of fumbling clothes later, and I was sliding inside her wet heat, swallowing her moans into my mouth. Her fingers fisted in my tuxedo jacket as she held me prisoner, putting me under her spell.

"I want," she panted, her body clenching me tight as she rolled her hips.

"What do you want, Cupcake? I'll give you whatever you want." And that was true. It was true four months ago. It was true three years ago, and it was true then.

"I want you to fuck me."

My whole body hummed with the need to make her come, to make her scream, to make her mine. Her lips found my cheek, my neck, her fingernails raked against my scalp, yanked at my jacket. She was pulling me into her, her "Please" so pretty on her lips.

I gripped her ass in one hand and pinned her hands above her head with the other, breathing in her moans as I drove into her, claiming her, making her mine. At the top of each thrust, she would clench around me, making me lose all sense.

Mine. All mine.

I let her wrists go, moving her in little circles as I thrust hard, pushing her until she was a mindless, hungry wild woman in my arms. When she sank her teeth into the side of my neck, I fought off the urge to do the same. I fought every single instinct I had to not end this torture right then and there.

Because Fiona was mine, but I would only truly make her so if she said yes.

Her release wrenched a gasp from her lips, the flush of her cheeks, her chest, that sexy-as-sin rosebud of a mouth, I'd never get enough. And when the violent bliss of my release slammed into me, I knew I'd gladly drown in her forever.

21

FIONA

Wrapped around Theo, I came back to myself. His scent filled my nose as I shakily slid my legs from his hips. And through the haze of what we had just done, did reality finally set in. Theo had just killed Hendrick.

And I'd let him.

I gripped Theo's jacket tight, looking up into those beautiful green eyes still shining with his wolf. I think it dawned on us right at that second that we were both royally screwed and not in the good way.

We were standing next to my ex's corpse, in my

father's house, where my engagement party was being held a floor below us.

Reality was a cold-hearted bitch.

"We need to get rid of the body."

Yes, that cold statement was the first thing that came out of my mouth. Not "What are we going to do?" Not "How the fuck do we get out of here?" Not "Oh, my God, I'm a horrible person." That last part was a total given. Because I could have stopped Theo.

I could have, but I didn't.

Hendrick's death was going to cause an arcane-wide incident. The Lanes had deep pockets and even deeper connections throughout the arcane community, and Hendrick was their precious baby boy. I'd known this the whole time. I'd known exactly who he was and how stupid it would be to kill him. I'd known, and I hadn't warned Theo. I didn't say, "Hey, maybe don't kill that guy."

Well, I had, but not with enough force to make Theo listen to me.

Because Hendrick had the gall to attack me in my own house—to hurt me not ten meters away from a party of witnesses. Anyone could have waltzed through that door and witnessed what he'd done. He touched me, and that signed his own death warrant.

Because not even my father would have let him get away with that.

"You didn't bring anything with you that you'd be upset to lose, did you?" Theo asked, pinching his brow and likely mapping out the logistics of trying to get my suitcase out of here.

"The only thing I'd be upset to lose is you in my life. Both of which are on the chopping block because of who that guy is," I hissed, gesturing to the bloody corpse at our feet.

The green that had faded from Theo's irises flared to life. "It doesn't matter who he was. He put his hands on you—"

"Yeah, yeah, yeah. I get it. He needed to die. Yes, I'm glad and appreciative, and it was fucking hot. Obviously, because we just fucked against that wall, but we need that body out of here, and we need a plan. Please, for the love of god."

His lips tipped up at my antics. "How did you get rid of the bodies in Savannah? Can't you do your witchy woo-woo and make him disappear?"

Theo Acosta did not just call intense entropy magic "witchy woo-woo." "I'm going to pretend you didn't say that and tell you that me using magic here is not a great idea."

He pursed his lips, staring at Hendrick's body. "I

didn't see him having any trouble with it."

"That is because he's a fucking moron, number one, and number two, he did have trouble. Hendrick is incredibly powerful. He was hamstrung by the wards in this place. It's why you only got tossed into a wall instead of disintegrated from the inside out."

Theo swiveled his gaze from me back to the body, his eyes wide. "Fair enough. Can you at least try? If he's powerful, you are a damn goddess. I recall you closing a Hell gate not twenty-four hours ago. If you put your mind to it, you can do anything."

And that was the problem, wasn't it?

I was scared to use my magic here. I was afraid to use my magic anywhere. All it had ever brought me was pain and more pain. My father used me, spells backfired, and a part of me wondered if the dark magic I'd absorbed to get this whole ball rolling was lurking somewhere inside of me.

"I'll be right here with you. No one's going to hurt you."

My laugh was mirthless. "And because you say it, you make it so. Is that how that works?"

"No," he said thoughtfully. "I've never been lucky a day in my life until the one you walked into it. We're going to make it out of this. Together. So close your eyes and concentrate."

Gritting my teeth, I slid my eyes closed and willed my body to perform the spell to make Hendrick disappear. Drawing on the power of those wards—the ones in every strut and support post, from the bones of arcaners in the mortar, of the ancestral well that sat below this home. I drew on it all, and when I opened my eyes, Hendrick was a pile of ash. Even that was fading away to nothing.

What the spell couldn't do, was steal the blood from Theo's skin or take away the bloody washrag Hendrick had been using to clean the scratches on his face.

"Wash your hands. Get the blood off of you. We need to get the fuck out of here before somebody realizes we aren't the only ones that are missing."

Theo did as told, scrubbing his hands clean in the bathroom before snatching the bloody rag from the floor and attempting to stuff it in his pocket.

"Absolutely not," I hissed, stealing it from his hands. With a snap of my fingers, the washcloth ignited, and I tossed it into the fireplace, watching it burn to ash as well.

"Well, that's one problem taken care of. You got a plan for getting us out of here, too, or is that my job?" he asked, his eyebrow raised in that sardonic way that made me want to both kiss the shit out of him and punch him in the balls.

"Well, it's not like I can just draw a portal in this

bitch. And I'm pretty sure there are enough guards surrounding this place that stealing a vehicle is probably out."

"Why can't you draw a portal?" he asked, and it was a valid question but one I was hesitant to answer.

Pinching my brow, I blamed the wards instead of my own fear. The last time I created a portal, it went straight to Hell. I couldn't exactly see myself trying out that particular spell anytime soon.

Theo grabbed me by the waist, drawing me in, making me look at him. "You know I can smell the lie in that, right? You're scared. It's okay to be scared. If you don't think you can do a portal, just tell me that."

He was right. Now was not the time to lie to him. "I don't think I can open the portal without fucking it up. There, I said it. You happy? Plus, the wards here are crazy, and I don't know if they're tuned to me anymore. I don't know anything anymore. I knew my father was fucked up, but he just tried to sell me off to my shitty ex-boyfriend for... I don't even know what."

"I still can't believe you dated that fuckhead."

"Yeah, it was a shining moment in the absolute train wreck of my past. Thank you."

Theo's lips tipped up. "Welcome. Now we can't do a portal, and we can't make a break for it. What's door number three?"

Door number three was a teensy tiny little artifact heist. A forbidden artifact heist, to be exact. "Have you ever heard of a transportation orb?"

I'd never regretted a dress so fast in my life. While perfect for a soiree of any kind, this backless cloud of a dress would get me in a shit-ton of trouble. Somehow, we needed to get to my father's office without alerting a single guard or party guest or being seen by anyone at all. Ever.

Piece of cake.

There were servants' corridors all over the place, but with the party going on, it was possible that we'd run into someone. Our best bet was to glamour our facial features, and hopefully, no one would remember my dress. I gave Theo mousy brown hair, a squat nose, and a soft chin while gifting myself dishwater blonde hair in a slightly pinched face.

Threading my arm around his, I ducked my head whenever we passed someone. Even with all the drama, the party was still going strong. It was as if Hendrick and I would come back in, saying, "Just kidding," and the night would go off without a hitch.

I had to hand it to my mother. She was the optimist.

Getting upstairs was the actual test. My father's guards were positioned at the bottom and top landings, walking back and forth like they expected a hit on his office.

Getting rid of the bottom guard was easy. All I had to do was set a guy's tuxedo on fire. Before I get the judgment, Atticus Garrett was a well-known philanderer, cheating on four of his six ex-wives and never visiting his children. Plus, the guard put him out within thirty seconds.

Thirty seconds we needed.

In the middle of the commotion, the lower and upper guards were paying so much attention to what was going down that Theo and I managed to slip past them, racing up the stairs on Theo's swift legs.

Unfortunately, that didn't stop my father's office from being guarded by four more witches.

A long time ago, I'd used sweetening spells, little bits of magic that got me whatever I wanted. Too bad they didn't typically work on members of my own coven— that was if I even *was* a member of the Jacobs Coven anymore.

"Unless we want to beat the shit out of these guys, I need to spell them," I whispered in Theo's ear, trying not to alert them to our presence.

"It's only four witches, Cupcake. How bad could it be?" he murmured back.

As dangerous as the situation was, his confidence

brought me hope. "You know this is risky. If we get caught—"

"We're not going to get caught." He cut me off before dropping a kiss on my lips. "And if we do, hopefully, I'll hit them hard enough that they forget who they saw."

Okay. You can do this.

"Stay behind me, and don't do anything crazy."

Theo put a hand to his chest in a "Who, me?" gesture. Like he wasn't the epitome of crazy. Not that I could talk...

Taking a deep breath, I left the alcove, marching straight for the witches with my altered face.

"Excuse me, ma'am," the first guard said, his face etched with purpose. "You can't be here. Guests are restricted to the first floor."

I let the sweetening spell I had used almost my entire life fill me, pressing it out as I broadened my smile. "Oh, well, aren't you just doing a fabulous job. I got lost on the way to the restroom. Could you help me out?"

His frown stayed put. "I'm sorry, ma'am. We can't leave our post. Please proceed downstairs. One of the guards will help you down there."

I put a hand on his arm, pressing more of the sweetening magic into him, trying to change his mind. "But can't *you* help me?"

The guard ripped my hand off him, shoving me away

as his eyes narrowed, alerting the other three guards that he had a major problem on his hands.

A spell whizzed past my head full of electricity and fire as a white wolf sailed past me, knocking a witch on his ass. I doubted Theo would kill them... Okay, so I *hoped* Theo wouldn't kill them.

The one he landed on stayed immobile, knocked out when his head hit the ground. Then he was on the other two, dodging spells as he used his big body and brute force to take them out. With nothing for it, I shot a Taser-like stunning spell into the first witch, electrocuting him just a teensy bit.

Okay, so, he wet himself and wouldn't shit right for a week, but I was desperate.

With the four guards incapacitated, I did the thing I really didn't want to do.

The thing I hadn't quite told Theo about.

The thing that would come and bite us—or me—in the ass.

The only person who could open my father's door was Josiah Jacobs himself. This particular entrance was spelled, biometrically encoded just for him. If I wanted in that door, I'd either have to go through the wall beside it —which was nearly impossible—or blow this motherfucker to smithereens.

Guess which one I chose.

"Stand back," I ordered, gathering my magic.

But I didn't just gather my magic. I also sipped the magic of the witches unconscious at my feet. They weren't dead, but they could lend me a little while I was here. When I thought I had enough, I blew that door to pieces.

Wood shards flew in every direction, embedding in the walls and the floor, but none of them touched us. I made sure of it. With that obstacle out of the way, I raced to the safe hidden in the bookcase behind my father's desk.

No, this was not my first artifact heist, nor was it even my fifth. It was just I didn't typically steal from my own father.

As smart as my father was, he didn't look at the details. Sure, his office was locked with spells that would alert him the second we got through, but he never really considered spelling the safe behind his desk.

He thought his wardings were enough.

Rookie.

A snap of my fingers later, the safe opened, and I closed my fist around a bright-blue transportation orb. Transportation orbs had been banned in the twelfth century. Mainly because they had a *terrible* habit of making the user explode into a million pieces if the math was even slightly wrong.

They were one of the few banned items in the arcane world. This wasn't the first time I had stolen one of these things, and the ABI knew my father had them. Unless they had conducted a raid in the last three years, he had a slew more tucked away somewhere.

He could spare this one.

Reconfiguring the math in my head, I pointed us to Savannah, readying the orb for the both of us. It was nearly done when the thunder of footsteps broke my concentration. My father and Paul were at the doorway, my father's face bright purple with rage as I activated the orb.

"Don't you da—"

"Hang on to me," I ordered Theo, ignoring my father and breathing easy for the first time all day as he wrapped his arms around my middle.

"Don't move," I insisted, shoving us through space and time.

I knew I would never return of my own free will. I also knew that if my father ever loved me at all, he'd forget he'd ever seen me here.

But as we ripped ourselves away from his office, I knew he would never let this go.

I was sure of it.

22

THEO

If I ever heard the words "transportation orb" again, I was going to gut someone. When Fiona suggested traveling this way, I'd thought it would be easy. No one said shit about how much it was going to feel like my skin was getting peeled from my bones, or how sick it would make us, or that this method of travel was suspect at best.

The orb dumped us in a wooded area that I hoped was far away from the Jacobs Coven. I landed flat on my back with Fiona on top of me, somehow shielding her from the ground underneath. When she caught her breath, she eventually rolled off me into the grass, the singed trees and foliage still smoldering from our landing.

"Where the fuck are we?" I growled, getting to my feet as the world finally righted itself. I held out a hand, and she took it, pulling herself up.

"Forsyth Park, the outskirts of one of the hidden places."

I had lived in Savannah my whole life—nearly one hundred and ten years of it—and I had never been to this part of Forsyth Park. "Are you sure?"

Fiona waggled a hand at me. "About seventy-thirty. I didn't have time to check my math, but this is where I was aiming for, and we didn't blow up, so I'm considering it a win." She powered down the orb, the blue light fading before she buried it in the earth.

"A lot of the witches had hidden ancestral wells here. When all of the descendants of a line die, their ancestral well opens up, revealing itself. I may have aided the end of a line months ago near here," she admitted, shame coloring her expression for a moment before she cleared it. "If we head west, we'll get to the rest of the park."

"Far be it from me to doubt a witch's sense of direction." I held out my hand, taking Fiona's in mine and guiding us out of the space. It took about half an hour, but we finally made it to Forsyth Park proper, the wide-open green spanning the distance between the witch side of town and the shifter.

On our way to my home, I couldn't help but feel a little shell-shocked. Fiona had held her own. She had gotten us out of there, but I had no illusions that Josiah would let this go. If anything, his daughter's defiance would toss a grenade on their relationship.

And honestly, it couldn't have happened to a nicer guy.

By the time we reached my house, my phone was having a small stroke in my pocket, Nico's number flashing every thirty seconds or so. I had a feeling things were about to go sideways. Then again, at least no one knew about Hendrick... *yet*.

"If you keep ignoring him, he's going to find more creative ways of calling you home," Fiona warned, unzipping her dress as soon as we hit my bedroom.

My whole body drew tight as I watched her slide from the fabric, with only a pair of lacy underwear covering her sexy ass.

"I'll ignore him as long as you're dressed like that," I answered, prowling across the room to pull her into my arms.

Then the reality of what had just happened hit me.

Fiona was in danger because of what I'd done. Her father would want retribution. So would the coven he sold her to. The only way out of this was to give her my protection—the only bargaining chip I had in this mess.

"I should give you my bite," I murmured, bringing her bruised wrist to my lips, kissing away that fucker's touch. "Nico says you're pack, but... mates are protected, revered. If I—"

Fiona's gaze locked on mine as she put a finger to my lips. "That is permanent. If we—if you did that, you'd be stuck... with *me*. You could—"

This time it was my turn to shut her up.

"Die without love because of circumstance? Miss out on years with someone who makes me want to live? Wolves might get their mates chosen for them, but it would be no sacrifice to choose you. And if my bite gives you the protection you need I... I-I need you safe, Fiona. I need you with me. I... need you."

Her cornflower-blue eyes warmed, a slow grin dawning on her face. "If I recall, someone said that I was yours. I think," she murmured, dropping a kiss to my shoulder, "that person was you."

Mine. All mine.

Scooping her up, I deposited us on my bed, still ignoring the buzzing of my phone. But a moment later, a scream ripped from her lips, tearing through every bit of happiness we'd just gained.

She scrambled away, her arm held out from her body

as a message began etching itself into her skin, the dark magic making me helpless as she writhed in pain.

This is war. Your wolf can't save you from me.

Josiah Jacobs had fired the first shot in a war that had been brewing for a decade.

And I was going to make that bastard pay.

The scent of searing flesh had me guiding her to the bathroom so I could get her arm under the cool spray. Tears streaming down her face, Fiona whispered words of healing, but the declaration of war did not fade.

"We need to call Nico," I growled, ready and willing to commit another murder today. "But first, you need to say yes to me."

Fiona curled into my arms as she slowly nodded.

Moments later, I met her gaze as my fangs sliced into the skin of her uninjured wrist, the coppery tang of her blood filling my mouth as I gave her my mark. Her blue eyes flared with magic as the flesh instantly healed into a shimmering scar.

This gave Fiona every protection of the Acosta pack as if she had been born into it. As if she had always been the one Fate had chosen for me.

She would be safe.

I just had to tell my brother first.

Thank you so much for reading Curses & Chaos. I can't express just how much I love Fiona & Theo and their ragtag bunch of friends. And we aren't quite done yet!

*However, if you would love to see a special glimpse of Fiona & Theo's first meeting from HIS point of view, turn the page for an epic **Lost Witch Bonus Scene**. I hope you enjoy it!*

*Next up is **Hexes & Hijinx** and all the crazy, witchy shenanigans that is to come. I hope you're buckled in to see Fiona & Theo contend with Fiona's family, a boatload of revenge... oh, and their crazy mate bond!*

Want the skinny on future releases without having to follow me absolutely everywhere on social media?
Text "LEGION" to (844) 311-5791

BONUS SCENE

Dear Reader,

I hope you enjoyed Curses & Chaos. Fiona & Theo have a very special place in my heart, and I am absolutely ecstatic for you to read more about her and her favorite wolf.

I have an extra special bonus scene for you as a thank you for reading. All you have to do is click the link below, sign up for my newsletter, and you'll get an email giving you access!

SIGN UP HERE:
https://geni.us/cc-bonus

HEXES & HIJINX

The Lost Witch Book Two

I went against the Coven. What's the worst that could happen?

When your dad is the head of the most notorious arcane crime family in the country, telling him no isn't really in the cards. My rebellion has brought the promise of war on the horizon, and the last thing Savannah needs is my mob boss father in the mix.

But if they find out my fiance is dead? And the Alpha's second killed him? Well, Theo's bite won't be able to save us.

Nothing will.

Preorder Hexes & Hijinx today!

Want more in the Arcane Souls World? Check out...

DEAD TO ME

Grave Talker Book One

Meet Darby. Coffee addict. Homicide detective. Oh, and she can see ghosts, too.

There are only three rules in Darby Adler's life.
One: Don't talk to the dead in front of the living.
Two: Stay off the Arcane Bureau of Investigation's radar.
Three: Don't forget rules one and two.

With a murderer desperate for Darby's attention and an ABI agent in town, things are about to get mighty interesting in Haunted Peak, TN.

Grab Dead to Me today!

Want more in the Arcane Souls World? Check out...

NIGHT WATCH

Soul Reader Book One

Waking up at the foot of your own grave is no picnic... especially when you can't remember how you got there.

There are only two things Sloane knows for certain: how to kill bad guys, and that something awful turned her into a monster. With a price on her head and nowhere to run, choosing between a job and a bed or certain death sort of seems like a no-brainer.

If only there wasn't that silly rule about not killing people...

Grab Night Watch today!

To stay up to date on all things Annie Anderson, get exclusive access to ARCs and giveaways, and be a member of a fun, positive, drama-free space, join The Legion!

facebook.com/groups/ThePhoenixLegion

ACKNOWLEDGMENTS

A huge, honking thank you to Shawn, Barb, Jade, Angela, Heather, Kelly, Erin, and April. Thanks for the late-night calls, the endurance of my whining, the incessant plotting sessions, the wine runs…

Basically, thanks for putting up with my bullshit.

Every single one of you rock and I couldn't have done it without you.

ABOUT THE AUTHOR

Annie Anderson is the author of the international bestselling Rogue Ethereal series. A United States Air Force veteran, Annie pens fast-paced Urban Fantasy novels filled with strong, snarky heroines and a boatload of magic. When she takes a break from writing, she can be found binge-watching The Magicians, flirting with her husband, wrangling children, or bribing her cantankerous dogs to go on a walk.

To find out more about Annie and her books, visit www.annieande.com

facebook.com/AuthorAnnieAnderson

twitter.com/AnnieAnde

instagram.com/AnnieAnde

amazon.com/author/annieande

bookbub.com/authors/annie-anderson

goodreads.com/AnnieAnde

pinterest.com/annieande

tiktok.com/@authorannieanderson

patreon.com/annieanderson